Echoes of the Past

by

Emma Kaye

The Lobster Cove Series

Echoes of the Past

Cover Art by *RJ Morris*

The Wild Rose Press, Inc.
PO Box 708
Adams Basin, NY 14410-0708
Visit us at www.thewildrosepress.com

Publishing History
First Fantasy Rose Edition, 2015
Print ISBN 978-1-5092-0517-2
Digital ISBN 978-1-5092-0454-0

The Lobster Cove Series
Published in the United States of America

"I have a second bedroom. Why don't you stay with me?" It wouldn't hurt to get in good with her new landlord. And if he planned to fix up the second floor and move in, it would be a good idea to make friends.

What would he wear to bed? The modern half of her hoped he was a boxers only kind of man. She wouldn't mind having the eye candy around. Her shy, seventeenth-century half prayed for smelly, disgusting nightclothes that covered every inch of his body. She didn't need the temptation so close at hand. Hitting on her new landlord was likely a bad idea.

He studied her for a second. He seemed like the kind of guy to weigh all his options. Stanley had always said Gray was a careful boy, begging the question of why he'd come all this way without knowing the true state of affairs.

He cleaned his glasses once again. With his face tilted down in concentration, he said, "Thanks. I'd appreciate that."

"Well, okay then."

Havoc loped over to her side and shoved his nose under her hand. He approved, apparently. But he didn't have to worry about exposing his secret life as her familiar, did he? No big deal for the dog.

For her, on the other hand, letting her secret out could be disastrous. She'd tried having a roommate once upon a time. The situation hadn't worked out well at all. Even in these modern times no one looked kindly on finding a witch in their midst.

Dear lord, what had she just agreed to?

Kudos to Emma Kaye

Ms. Kaye's debut novel with The Wild Rose Press,
TIME FOR LOVE,
has more than fifty Amazon.com reviews
averaging 4.4 out of 5 stars.
~*~
It was a finalist in the NJRW Golden Leaf contest.

Dedications

To my family—I love you, through all time.
Your love is the magic that keeps me going.
~*~
To my critique partners—Ruth A. Casie, Lita Harris,
Nicole S. Patrick, Julie Rowe and DC Stone—Thank
you for your never-ending encouragement and support.
~*~
To Claudia Fallon
and everyone at The Wild Rose Press,
I've loved working with you all.
Thanks for everything you do to make each project
a success.

Prologue

Settlement of L'Anse des Homards, Maine, 1692

Fire licked at the wood piled below Isabeau Munier. The heat overwhelmed her. She barely remembered the spell she'd so carefully prepared while imprisoned in the tavern's root cellar. Black spots floated across her vision. She fought to remain conscious.

A string of crude curses she'd overheard while awaiting her sentence burst unintentionally from her lips. Coarse rope scratched her arms as she thrashed back and forth, struggling to escape the flames so close to her hem. If the fire reached her clothing, she'd be engulfed in an instant.

Smoke clogged her lungs, but a hint of the sage Heloise had sprinkled upon the wood recalled her to her senses. Hopefully, long enough to make good her escape. Heloise worked her way clockwise through the crowd around the pyre. Silver sparkles shimmered through the air as she completed the path that closed the magick circle.

Merci!

She sent a silent prayer of thanks for Heloise's quick work. Finally, all was in place so she could recite the spell. And not a moment too soon.

She whispered the words, trusting the smoke to

hide the movement of her lips but worried her voice might carry through the air to those eager to hear her screams. Heloise's *maman* would likely stone her if she suspected what Isabeau attempted. The crowd wanted blood and the smell of burning flesh to whet their appetites for the feast they'd share this evening in celebration of burning a witch.

Searing pain arced through her throat as she struggled to complete the words. Each breath brought an agony of scorching heat. Dizziness threatened, but the ropes locked her in place.

> *"Hear these words, hear my cry,*
> *spirits from the other side.*
> *I seek your help as one who tries*
> *to do no harm and tell no lies.*
> *I have been wronged but place no blame,*
> *please protect me from the flames.*
> *I wish to leave, I can not stay,*
> *send me somewhere far away.*
> *I've had my say, you've heard my plea,*
> *if it please, so mote it be."*

The last of the spell came out on a gasping cough. A dark force pressed against her. Something wasn't right, but her muddled mind couldn't make out from where the feeling came. In her panic, had she misstated the spell?

The fire caught, roared up around her. She cringed in anticipation of fire scorching her skin.

Nothing. The flames didn't touch her. An invisible wall blocked their heat. Light dazzled her eyes. A cool breeze caressed her body and relief forced a laugh out of her. Her legs sagged. The ropes kept her upright, but they no longer caused her any pain. Her lungs were raw, but the air she breathed contained life rather than death.

The crowd's jeering faces faded into the background. Her last sight was of their jaws dropping in shock. Their faces transformed into a wavering mass of color. She could no longer distinguish Madame Talbert's pinched, weasel-like face from Monsieur Figard's fat, bloated pig snout.

She shouted her triumph. The "good" people of L'Anse des Homards had failed. She'd escaped this godforsaken town and she'd never be back.

Chapter One

Lobster Cove, Maine, Present Day

Isabeau contemplated the solid mass of black and white fur that blocked her view of the room. The giant dog had plopped into her lap a mere second after she'd taken a seat on the worn-out old sofa at April Showers Pet Rescue—otherwise known as April's house. Isabeau's best friend worked with Dr. Foster from Old Mill Vet to find homes for abandoned animals.

April had said Isabeau needed to meet her latest charge to believe him. And she was right about that. The monstrous harlequin Great Dane outweighed her by about forty pounds if April hadn't underestimated the beast's weight of one hundred seventy pounds.

She petted the sleek spotted back. The dog's front legs were still on the floor, but with his butt in her lap, his pointy ears towered above her. He'd be intimidating if he weren't so sweet.

"Killer? Really?" She couldn't think of a more inappropriate name for the gentle giant.

"The previous owner was a bit of an ass," April responded.

"I can imagine. I find it hard to understand how anyone could give up such a love." Killer tilted his head back and stared at her with his sweet puppydog eyes.

April dropped onto the couch next to them. "I'm so

happy to hear you say that."

Isabeau frowned in suspicion. "Why?"

"You said you were thinking of getting a pet."

Isabeau scratched Killer behind the ear. He leaned into her hand with a funny-sounding moan of pleasure. "Oh, you like that, do you?" she asked in a singsong baby voice.

Zut alors.

The connection was undeniable. Fate had seen fit to provide her with a familiar. She was taking him home. "I had rather pictured a cat—my apologies, Killer—but you're right. A dog shall do much better. No one will dare break into Cove Secrets now."

April laughed. "Was that actually a concern? I didn't think you even bothered to lock up at night, let alone worry someone might break into your shop."

Isabeau curled her lip. "*Vraiment.* Lobster Cove is no longer the den of sin and vice it once was, is it?"

Killer dropped down to lie across both their laps. April grunted as his head landed across her thighs. "It's peaceful here. Your motorcycle's the loudest thing around."

Isabeau smiled at the thought of the Suzuki Savage 650 sitting under its cover beside her home. Good thing she'd walked over. Killer would never fit across the handlebars.

The bike gave her a freedom she'd rarely known in her life, even if she couldn't leave Hancock County without triggering her curse. Her home had enough winding roads to make it fun, if limited. In her old life, she'd never even been on a horse that could manage anything faster than a walk. The local washerwoman's teenage daughter had no reason to go for a gallop, even if they could possibly have afforded anything more than a sway-backed old mule.

"I can't call him Killer. *Son nom est...*" He shifted his gaze, and she stared into his big brown eyes until it came to her. "Havoc. His name is Havoc." Not a name she'd have chosen, but it wasn't her call. She fingered Havoc's frayed rope collar. "I will have to do a little shopping. That collar will not do. Havoc has an image to maintain as security guard for Cove Secrets. Maybe something tie-dyed."

She loved tie-dye. She'd spent a year in the sixties before moving on and finally settling in this decade. That had been her first stop, and when she'd gotten over the shock that her spell had taken her to another time rather than place, she'd thought to stay there for the rest of her days. But the spell had other plans.

She'd hopped back and forth through time ever since.

This time had been her home longer than any other. Genius that she was, it had taken her a number of time shifts before she figured out she couldn't cross the county line without getting tossed through time. There were a few other areas she couldn't approach as well, but she believed she'd mapped them all out by now.

Not that she'd had much choice, but this century was much better than many others she'd suffered through. And she'd learned to love it. True, she had issues with a few people here, and her dream of traveling the world would never be a reality, but she wouldn't trade her little store for anything.

She loved the wacky array of products she sold to the tourists that flocked to Lobster Cove each summer. From twisted-wire lobster claw earrings, made by a local mother of three, to delicate glass-blown ornaments, to dog biscuits baked by her friend April, Cove Secrets carried a little bit of everything. As long as something caught her eye and she didn't see duplicates in every store along the waterfront, she wanted it. And when business slowed during the deep snows of winter, she enjoyed nothing more than curling up with a good book—like the latest romance by local author Scarlette LaFlamme, a roaring fire, and the view of the mountains out her living room window.

Male companionship would have been nice, but with her curse hanging over her head, she had to accept that romantic involvement was not in the cards for her. Havoc would fill the small void in her life she'd only vaguely realized was there. He could curl up beside her on her sofa while she read and keep her company when she went on her daily walks.

Yes. Havoc would fit perfectly into her life. She would simply ignore the small voice in her ear that wished for more.

****

Grayson Wright parked his rented sedan next to the curb in front of the Evard house. Would Sherri be there? He glanced at his watch. One-thirty. She could be at work. He had no idea what she'd been up to lately. They'd drifted apart shortly after she got married. He hadn't seen her in sixteen years.

He probably should have dropped his things off at the house, but he'd decided to look up his old high school girlfriend first. He'd completely severed ties with anything Lobster Cove the second he was able. Sherri was the only one he regretted ignoring.

He hoped Uncle Stan had been right about Sherri

moving back home to take care of her mom. He peeked out the passenger window for a quick glance at the house.

Pretty much the same. There might have been a fresh coat of paint at some point, but what must have once been a vibrant yellow was now as faded as he remembered. An old wooden picnic table took up most of the small front yard. Its large green umbrella listed to the side, adding to the slightly run-down aspect of the home.

Blue and white flowered curtains on either side of the open bow window fluttered in the breeze. If he angled his head, he just might be able to get a glimpse inside.

Yes. There she was, or at least, there was the shadow of someone walking by. He hoped it was Sherri, and not her mother. He'd never gotten along all that well with Sherri's parents. A poor kid from the wrong side of town could never be good enough for their daughter. What would they think of him now? His financial consulting firm was booming and his clients were among the wealthiest people in the world. He could retire tomorrow without a care in the world. The days of scrounging for dinner were long past.

He shrugged the memories aside and locked his glove compartment. He'd have to find a better place to store Uncle Stan's paperwork, but for now, the glove compartment would have to do. If he had time, he'd swing by the bank to rent a safe deposit box.

He whistled to himself as a hot blonde crossed the street walking an enormous black and white spotted dog. She didn't seem strong enough to handle such a monster, but the two were perfectly in step as they sashayed down the avenue. Maybe he'd ask Sherri if she knew how he could track down the blonde. Small towns like this were notorious for knowing everybody's business. Sometimes that could work in his favor.

She turned down a side street and he lost sight of the duo. Nice to know the town had some new life in it since he'd left.

The car door took more force than he was used to. He shoved harder and it snapped closed with a *bang*. Damn, he missed his 'Vette. But he wanted to stay inconspicuous on this trip. And the 'Vette was anything but.

He sauntered up the front stoop and rang the doorbell.

"Be with you in a moment," Sherri called out.

Gray wandered around as he waited for her to answer the door. He wanted a closer look at that picnic table. A smile tugged at his mouth when he found the heart cut into the top. *GW + SE* jaggedly carved in the center. Sherri's mom had nearly whipped his ass when she'd noticed. But he'd gotten to third base with Sherri that night in his beat-up old truck, so he'd considered it well worth it.

"Can I help you?"

He looked up and met Sherri's gaze through the screen door.

She tilted her head, her brows scrunched in concentration. Then her eyes widened and a huge grin transformed her expression. "Gray!" She shoved the door open with a squeal, her very pregnant belly preceding her by a long shot.

He rushed to meet her halfway, his arms wide to embrace as much of her as he could. "Whoa, Sherri!

Uncle Stan never mentioned you were pregnant. When's the baby due?"

She pulled back with a frown. "What baby?"

Heat exploded all over him. He opened his mouth, but had no idea what to say.

Shit.

She burst into a giggling fit and lightly punched him on the arm. "I'm joking. She's due in about two months, but my first was two weeks late, so I'm not holding out hope that she'll be on time." She rubbed her belly, a fond smile on her face.

Relief flooded through him. "Bitch. That was a dirty trick." Humor laced his words. He'd see just how much she'd changed in a minute.

She smiled. "You deserved it, you rat-bastard."

"Same ol' Sherri. Foul-mouthed as ever."

She shrugged. "I have to tone it down most days. My daughter's seven. She picks up on everything," she said, rolling her eyes.

"Your mom would say, 'Payback's a bitch.' "

Sherri's smile faded. "I lost Mom a year ago." She sniffed and swiped at the corner of her eye. "I was really sorry to hear about your uncle."

His chest tightened. She'd always been so close to her mother. The loss would have been extremely tough on her. So many memories. Coming back here would be even harder than he'd thought. And Uncle Stan was such a huge part of that.

She cleared her throat. "So are you here for a while, or just wrapping up some of Stan's business before scooting back down to your big, fancy New York City life?"

He rubbed the back of his neck and gave her a

sideways glance. "Actually, I'm thinking about staying in town for a while."

Astonishment clouded her gaze. "You're shitting me. I thought you hated it here. After…"

Thankfully, she let that sentence trail off. He had no desire to rehash *those* old times. Bad enough driving into town down the street where… He didn't need to talk about that shit. "I need a change for a while. I figured here's as good a place as any other." And with all the turmoil over Uncle Stan's will he was in no mood to add apartment hunting to his to-do list. But he was also getting sick of the hotel he'd been staying at since breaking up with Lisa. He'd been there long enough.

"Well, we should get together. I can show you all that's changed since we were kids. Where are you staying?"

"You know Uncle Stan's house over on Elm Avenue? I figured I'd stay there."

She stiffened, but then a satisfied smirk settled on her face. "So he didn't leave it to *her* after all." She crossed her arms on top of her enormous stomach.

"Her?" He knew exactly who, but he'd gotten the impression Uncle Stan's tenant was an old friend, certainly not someone to raise such animosity.

"That gold-digging bitch who runs Cove Secrets. She's been trying to latch onto Stan since she showed up here from out of nowhere a few years ago."

He gave a short bark of laughter. "Someone's been trying to land Uncle Stan?" The idea was ludicrous, but he wasn't amused. He knew all too well what women would do when they smelled a gravy train.

"Oh, she's horrible. Stan set her up in his place,

helped her open up a store in town and everything. It's like she put some kind of spell on him." She made the sign of the cross and shuddered.

He raised an eyebrow.

"I'm serious. She's a witch. She works her magick at midnight, with dark candles and strange-colored smoke. I've also seen her wandering the nature trails collecting poisonous mushrooms." She folded her arms protectively over her belly. "Be careful when you kick her out. She might curse you. And don't eat anything she tries to serve you."

He scoffed at the notion. "Don't be absurd. There're no such things as witches. And what are you doing watching her at midnight, anyway?"

She had the grace to blush. "It was shortly after she showed up. I saw her through her window because she hadn't hung any curtains yet."

As curious and suspicious as ever apparently. Some of the reasons he'd broken up with her in high school came rushing back.

"You just happened past her window?" The house wasn't exactly next door. No way Sherri strolled by in the middle of the night by accident.

She grinned, shrugged, and changed the subject.

They chatted a few more minutes until Sherri left to pick her daughter up from Lobster Cove Elementary.

As he started up the piece-of-shit rental and then drove down Ash Avenue, memories—good and bad—weighed him down.

****

Isabeau introduced Havoc to his new home by letting him loose in the shop first. Impressive. Had her displays been placed any lower he'd have swept her clear of inventory with the first swipe of his huge tail. Thankfully, his enthusiastic wagging hit below her countertops and did no damage. He inspected everything, paying particular attention to a basket of stuffed animals before snatching a mouthful of dog biscuits, then returning to her side to sit on her toes.

She laughed. "Seriously, *mon chien*? Is the floor too cold for your precious little bottom?"

The bell rang as someone pushed open the front door. Havoc's ears perked, but he stayed put. Interesting. What kind of guard dog would he make? Not a very good one if the *thump, thump* of his tail hitting her leg was any indication. Given she ran a retail store, that probably wasn't a bad thing. She didn't need the giant dog attacking the paying customers.

"Good afternoon! Let me know if I can help you with anything," she called out. The sun streaming through the window cast him in shadow. She couldn't get a good look at his face, but he was tall and appeared well built. Light glinted off glasses.

He stepped forward out of the shadows. His navy blue suit and red striped tie spoke of a city, rather than her small town. A tourist then, but one in town on business. A cute businessman. She liked his short, dark brown hair and the way the black frames of his glasses enhanced rather than detracted from his face.

"Are you shopping for anything in particular? A gift, perhaps?"

He shook his head and continued toward her, his hand outstretched. "Are you Isabeau Munier?"

Havoc stepped between them, closing the distance in one long stride.

The stranger's eyes widened behind his lenses but

he held his ground and said in his deep baritone voice, "Sit."

Havoc promptly dropped to his haunches, his tongue lolled out and he nuzzled the stranger's hand.

"Good…boy?"

"*Oui.* Yes." She rushed forward and grabbed Havoc's collar. She'd given him a nice red and white patterned cloth collar with a silver dog bone nameplate. "I apologize. He appears to like you, though." One point in the tourist's favor. She'd always found animals to be the best judges of character. "You were looking for me?"

"Yes. I'm Gray Wright. Stan's nephew."

She smiled. "How nice! Are you here with your uncle? Dear Stanley, such a sweet man. I've been expecting him to visit any day now. My rent is due."

He rubbed the back of his neck, appearing ill at ease. "You don't know." He took a deep breath. "I'm sorry to inform you Uncle Stan passed away last week."

****

Isabeau's stomach dropped. She fell against the counter, sending a white porcelain teapot crashing to the ground. She could picture Stanley the day she first met him. She'd been disoriented, to say the least, having just time traveled for the first time.

He'd been a young, attractive man back then. He took her hand and helped her up from where she'd stumbled to a heap at his feet. His attention flustered the sixteen-year-old who'd just escaped a would-be execution. Young women in her time weren't supposed to talk to men they didn't know. Not without a chaperone. The lack of someone to look after her reputation had been what almost got her killed in the first place.

Havoc's deep-throated whine brought her back to the present. Stanley's nephew probably thought she was insane. Her reaction was a bit much over the death of someone he'd see as just her landlord. If he only knew.

She knelt and began picking up shards of porcelain. "I'm so sorry," she mumbled.

A strong, warm hand covered hers where it trembled over the mess she'd made. "Let me help. Why don't you keep the dog away; he might cut his paw. Do you have a dustpan?"

His eyes were a deep forest green behind his glasses. There was confusion in his gaze, but sympathy as well. Stanley had always spoken highly of his nephew. He'd tried to get her to agree to meet Gray on more than one occasion, but the situation had felt much too awkward given her history with his uncle.

Havoc nudged her in the neck, his cries softer now.

"Yes. Thank you."

She grabbed Havoc's collar and pulled him away from the debris. She clipped on a short leash and slipped it over a hook near the door before grabbing a dustpan and rushing to help.

The minute they took to clean passed in silence. The urge to speak bubbled up within her as the silence lengthened, but words escaped her.

She scraped the last of the debris into the garbage and returned the pan to its spot below the register before turning her attention fully to Stanley's nephew. Havoc had certainly taken to the man. The dog sucked up the attention as Gray scratched him behind the ears. Havoc was so tall, Gray didn't need to stoop at all to pet him. His focus was on the worshipful looks the dog lavished upon him so Isabeau took a moment to study the man she'd heard so much about.

Now that he was close up and not crouching to help her clean, she got a better sense of his height. She viewed herself as average at five foot six, and he towered over her. She tried not to gawk at his body so she lifted her gaze to his face, but it wasn't easy. She'd always enjoyed a man in a well-tailored suit. His fit him perfectly and he had the body type to go with it. Delightful.

She whipped around to straighten a display of crystals and stop her shameless ogling. What had gotten into her? She couldn't forget what he was doing here.

What *was* he doing here? He lived in Manhattan, if she recalled correctly. His uncle had often spoke of trying to get him to move out of the city and back to Lobster Cove where he'd grown up. He'd hinted something kept Gray out of town though, so why did he come back? Surely a phone call would have been enough.

She cleared her throat, bringing his attention off Havoc and back to her. When his hand stilled, Havoc bumped him with his nose. Gray continued his scratching, wise man.

"I'm sorry to hear about your uncle." Her voice cracked on the last word.

"Thank you." He ambled around the store near her, picking up knick-knacks, putting them back down, avoiding her gaze. "I assumed the lawyers would have called to inform you. And from your reaction to the news, I would guess you were closer to Uncle Stan than I thought."

"Why did you come all the way up here?" She felt

like a fool the minute the words were out of her mouth. Wasn't she a self-centered witch? He probably had lots of things to take care of in Lobster Cove. This wasn't his uncle's only property. "I'm sorry." She put a hand to her forehead. "I'm being terribly rude. It's just such a shock. It was very thoughtful of you to come. You must have a lot to deal with right now."

"That's okay. It came as quite a shock to me as well." He plucked his glasses off and cleaned the smudges with a cloth from an inside pocket of his suit jacket. "If you don't mind my asking, when was the last time you spoke with my uncle?"

She had to give it some thought. She chewed on her thumb, her teeth pulling at a slight rip in the nail, lengthening it so the entire edge became a jagged mess. "I think it was two months ago. He took me to The Cliffside for dinner. He wanted to talk to me about the second floor apartment."

"Ah, good." He let out a sigh and smiled. "Then he told you his plans to rent it out."

"That apartment?" She laughed. The second floor of the Cape Cod she rented on the outskirts of town was just a bit smaller than her two bedroom apartment on the first floor, but filled to bursting with just about everything Stanley had ever come across. Not to mention the lack of insulation or proper plumbing. "That would not be possible. It's a disaster up there. He told me he was thinking about hiring someone to clean it out." The urge to laugh left her abruptly. "Stanley always said it was a project he'd get to someday. And now he'll never get around to it. Is that why you're here? To clean out his things?"

Gray frowned. "No. I planned to move in."

Chapter Two

How many shocks would she have to suffer today?
"Move in? But—"

Gray held up a hand. "I was under the impression
the apartment had been taken care of. Obviously, it
slipped Uncle Stan's mind. He'd apparently been sick
for some time."

"He never said…" Why hadn't he told her? Tears
gathered in her eyes. She blinked rapidly to keep them
from falling.

"He never told me either." A muscle twitched
along his jawline, he clenched his teeth so tightly.

The pained tone of his voice made her wince. This
must be so much harder on him, Stanley had practically
raised him and his sister. She looked at her watch. "It's
almost closing time anyway. Let me lock up and we can
talk about this at the house." She glanced out the
window but didn't see a moving truck. Maybe he hadn't
meant he planned to move in now. He'd need to check
the place out, then arrange to move all his stuff. "Did
you have a few minutes or did you have someplace else
to be?"

He shook his head. "I made this my last stop
figuring I'd let you know I was here, then head over to
the house to spend the night." He rubbed the back of his
neck. "Shit. I'll run over to the Frenchman Bay Motel.
See if they have any vacancies."

She thought of the half marathon starting tomorrow. The crowds had already descended and rates at all the hotels had been raised to take advantage. Her shop had bustled with business earlier in the day before all the runners retired for an early night. She grimaced. "You'll be hard-pressed to find anything decent tonight."

Havoc plopped down on Gray's foot and leaned heavily against his side. Gray spread his legs to accommodate. Dogs were good judges of character. And Stanley had always raved about the boy, though boy wasn't a term she'd use for the man standing before her.

"I have a second bedroom. Why don't you stay with me?" It wouldn't hurt to get in good with her new landlord. And if he planned to fix up the second floor and move in, it would be a good idea to make friends.

What would he wear to bed? The modern half of her hoped he was a boxers only kind of man. She wouldn't mind having the eye candy around. Her shy, seventeenth-century half prayed for smelly, disgusting nightclothes that covered every inch of his body. She didn't need the temptation so close at hand. Hitting on her new landlord was likely a bad idea.

He studied her for a second. He seemed like the kind of guy to weigh all his options. Stanley had always said Gray was a careful boy, begging the question of why he'd come all this way without knowing the true state of affairs.

He cleaned his glasses once again. With his face tilted down in concentration, he said, "Thanks. I'd appreciate that."

"Well, okay then."

Havoc loped over to her side and shoved his nose under her hand. He approved, apparently. But he didn't have to worry about exposing his secret life as her familiar, did he? No big deal for the dog.

For her, on the other hand, letting her secret out could be disastrous. She'd tried having a roommate once upon a time. The situation hadn't worked out well at all. Even in these modern times no one looked kindly on finding a witch in their midst.

Dear lord, what had she just agreed to?

****

Gray popped the trunk on his rental and heaved both his duffle bags out, dropping them on the ground at his feet while he rooted around in the box of crap Lisa had tossed at him when he'd told her it was over. He'd flung his shaving kit in there somewhere…

Ah, yes. He spotted the strap and yanked it loose with one good tug. A few of his things spilled over into the trunk, but he let them be. He'd straighten it all out later. He still needed to go through everything and make sure nothing important was missing, although he hadn't kept anything he really cared about at their place. His favorite items were kept at the office. He could always buy a new television or coffee pot. A part of him must have known from the beginning it wasn't going to last.

Isabeau's shoulder brushed his leg as she bent beside him to grab one of his bags.

He stretched out a hand to stop her. "Here, I've got that." He hadn't realized she'd followed him out. Too busy wondering what the hell he'd been thinking when he agreed to stay, not only in the house, but in her apartment. He'd been surprised to find the blonde he'd been admiring earlier in the day was the same woman Sherri had warned him against. He hadn't been thinking straight then or now.

He fought an erection just watching her flip her long blond hair over her shoulder. What would he do if she was one of those women who strutted around the house practically naked? And if she were the gold-digger Sherri insisted, he'd bet his stock portfolio that's exactly what would happen.

"I insist." She smiled as she flung the heavy bag over her shoulder with ease.

She was one up on Lisa already. His ex wouldn't have even considered helping. Maybe Sherri was wrong. He hoped so. He'd hate to think Isabeau had taken advantage of his uncle's kind nature.

"So how long have you known Uncle Stan, anyway?"

Her gaze darted to the side and she bit her lip before she shrugged. "Oh, it seems like forever." She hitched the bag higher on her shoulder. "We should get you settled." She turned and headed down a short brick walk leading to the porch wrapped halfway round the small Cape Cod style house.

What was that all about?

He was pretty damn good at reading people, and the way she'd responded to his question, he'd swear she was keeping something back.

But what could she have to hide about meeting his uncle? The sinking feeling in his stomach gave credence to Sherri's gossip. Something was going on here.

****

Isabeau helped Gray haul his bags into the house.

He didn't have much. "Do you have a truck coming soon?" She plopped his bag on the bed in her guest room. The decor was a bit girly, but he was only staying temporarily, so hopefully it wouldn't be a big deal for him. Then again, maybe he'd like the huge roses on the comforter and the dried flowers in the vase on the nightstand. The collection of fancy perfume bottles might be a bit over the top though.

"No, I never cared about the furniture in my place. My ex picked it all. She can keep it."

She stared at him. "Really? How could you stand it? I hated it here until I got it decorated like I wanted."

He shrugged, the movement opening his jacket and revealing the long, lean lines of his torso. "I was barely ever there. It was basically a place to sleep when I wasn't working."

His jacket settled back into place and she tore her gaze away from his abdomen. Reluctantly. He hooked his thumbs in his belt, his hands hanging down to frame his crotch. Intentional? Probably not, but he certainly drew her attention to the area. She took a step back and bumped into the doorjamb. Heat suffused her cheeks. "Um, why don't you settle in here and I'll go fix us a little something to eat." Havoc brushed by her. "You too, Havoc."

She fled the room before he could notice how flustered she'd become. She'd left 1692 over fifteen years ago when she was only sixteen, but sometimes she still felt like the impressionable young maiden she'd once been. Then she recalled her best friend's fiancé—a well-respected merchant—who'd tried to rape her and claimed she was a witch when he got caught.

She'd grown up in a hurry after that.

She most definitely did not feel so unworldly now. Gray looked darn good in that suit and she fought a heavy dose of lust. A benefit of the times. If she were still the washerwoman's daughter, she'd have her backside whipped if anyone even suspected her of thinking such thoughts about a man. It had taken her a while to get used to it, but the free love movement of the sixties had given her a crash course in sexuality she wasn't soon to forget, even though she'd been too young at that time to fully embrace the idea.

She'd been lucky to meet a man like Gray's uncle. Someone who recognized the rebelliousness of a young girl experiencing her first taste of freedom and honorable enough not to take advantage. Or let anyone else do so. He'd saved her from making a number of mistakes when she first came forward in time.

She picked a framed photo of her and Stanley off her mantel. It was black and white and bent along the edges. She'd found it wedged in a desk drawer when Stanley first rented her the house. The nature of her curse made it difficult for her to hold on to mementos like this, so she'd been thrilled to find it. They were both so young in the picture. He'd been only twenty-four. Much too old for her teenage self, of course, but that hadn't kept her from having a rather large crush on him.

The door to the guest bedroom clicked shut.

Zut alors.

She couldn't have this photo around. What if Gray recognized her and his uncle? It was an impossible picture. She yanked open the drawer on a small pedestal table next to her overstuffed sofa and shoved the framed photo inside. She whirled around to find Gray—his brows raised—watching her from the hall.

She tucked her hair behind her ear and then gestured toward her small eat-in kitchen. "Are you hungry? I was just about to heat up some leftover Chinese."

"Sounds good."

He smiled. The first true smile he'd had since he'd walked into her store. She liked it.

Luckily, she always bought the quart size of everything when she had food delivered from Lucky Chan's. She'd never be able to eat at the restaurant since it was outside the county lines, but she didn't mind all that much. She liked the leftovers better than the fresh anyway.

She dished out two heaping portions of pork fried rice, beef lo mien and kung pao chicken and stuck them in the microwave, one on top of the other. She did so love the conveniences of modern times.

Gray watched her from the doorway.

She grabbed some sodas from the fridge and plunked the cans down on the table just as the microwave dinged. Gray beat her to it. He brought the plates over while she rummaged in her drawers for some matching silverware and paper napkins.

Just as her butt was about to hit the chair, Havoc whined and bumped his nose against her hand. "Oh, I'm sorry, Havoc." She scooted over to the monster bag of dog food April had recommended and measured four overflowing scoops of kibble into the raised dish she'd placed next to the refrigerator. To her surprise, Havoc didn't eat immediately. She frowned. "What's the matter?"

"Have you had him long?" Gray asked.

"No, actually. I just brought him home from the shelter today."

"He probably won't eat until we're done. He'll want to make sure he can't get anything better before he goes for his own food."

She settled into her seat across from him. "You appear to know a great deal about dogs."

"Had a few growing up." He shrugged. "But an old girlfriend had a Great Dane and she was a picky eater."

"The dog or the girlfriend?"

He chuckled. "Both."

She dug into her food and they ate in silence for a few moments. She'd been hungrier than she thought. Come to think of it, she'd skipped breakfast and lunch today, so caught up in her visit with April and then getting everything ready for Havoc. No wonder she was starving. Her eyes watered from a stray piece of hot pepper in the kung pao. A sip of soda did little to ease the fire, but a big bite of lo mien helped.

Havoc settled into a ball at her feet while they ate. Amazing how small he could curl himself up considering his size.

"How long have you lived here? Stan never mentioned you until…" He trailed off, then took a deep sip of his drink. "Well, until his last week or so. I'm afraid his mind was going in the end. He kept saying how he first met you when you were just a teenager—in 1964."

She understood the inflection in his voice. Indulgence for a crazy old man on his deathbed. He was partially justified. Stanley never would have given her secret away if he'd been in his right mind.

"About three years now." She'd sought Stanley out whenever she made a leap into a time period during his lifetime. This last had been quite a shock. He'd always been a strong, vital man. Three years ago, she'd been astonished to realize he'd grown old without her.

Gray swiped up the last of his lo mien, then fiddled with his fork as he chewed slowly. When he'd finished, he cleared his throat and opened his mouth once or twice as if trying to say something difficult.

She clenched her fists in her lap, his nervousness rubbing off on her. When he finally rested his fork on his plate, she leaped to take the dishes to the sink before he gathered his courage to say what was on his mind.

Something was up. And if it made Stanley's nephew this nervous, she wasn't sure she wanted to know what.

Chapter Three

Of course, Isabeau couldn't get away that easy. As she pumped soap onto her sponge to wash their dishes, Gray picked the drying towel off the handle of her stove and waited beside her.

He'd taken off his suit coat before dinner and rolled up his sleeves, revealing strong forearms sprinkled with dark hair. He unlatched his expensive-looking watch and tucked it into his pocket.

"Thanks for dinner."

"You are most welcome." She cast around for some reason to put a little distance between them. He was close enough to smell his cologne. She liked it a bit too much for good sense. "Perhaps you might like some coffee?" Their fingers brushed as she handed him the last dish. She had to force herself not to let go before he had a firm grasp, but it was difficult.

"Coffee would be great, thanks. Can I help?" he asked as he folded the towel neatly and replaced it exactly where he'd found it. Not in the same condition of course. How he managed to make the thing look so perfect when it was sopping wet, she had no idea. She never bothered to place it neatly, but just stuck the towel over the handle or, more often than not, tossed it onto the counter.

She shook her head. "No, thank you. If you'd have a seat in the living room, I can prepare your drink and bring it to you. There's barely enough room in this kitchen for the two of us. With Havoc here..." She glanced at the dog spread out in the middle of the room, making the space feel even smaller.

Gray replaced his watch as he strolled out of the kitchen after giving Havoc a quick pat. She breathed a sigh of relief. He seemed to have forgotten whatever issue had made him so nervous a few minutes ago. Maybe she'd get out of the evening without having to face some awfully awkward conversation. Talking to him made her blush, she didn't know how she'd manage a conversation that made *him* uncomfortable.

She used her large French press to make a batch of decaf for the two of them and poured the excess into a thermos for later. She hoped he didn't mind, but if she drank caffeine at this point in the night, she'd be up until the wee hours of the morn.

Her favorite mug wasn't fit for company, so she settled for the one with "Keep Calm and Call a Winchester" on it and a second with "I don't have ADHD, I just... Look a squirrel!" on it for him. Maybe he wouldn't have a sense of humor and she could forget about being attracted to him. That might come as something of a relief.

Alas, no. A grin pulled at the corner of his mouth when he read the saying. He didn't make any comment, just added a spoonful of sugar and a dash of cream. She did the same, then pushed Havoc to the side in order to gain a spot on her overstuffed couch.

Small talk had never been her strong suit, so they lapsed into silence. After a few minutes of quiet, Havoc swiveled around to watch her. She sighed as she read the message in the dog's eyes.

Get it over with.

If she'd had any doubt that the dog was her familiar, it faded away in that instant. The sense of knowing what the dog wanted from her was too strong.

Havoc continued to stare at her.

All right, all right, she thought to the dog, who let out a sigh and dropped his head in her lap. "Pray tell me why you have elected to move home to Lobster Cove after all this time. Your uncle despaired of ever having you return." She bit her lip. Poor choice of words. She hadn't meant to make him feel bad about moving home too late.

He didn't appear to notice her slip. At least, he didn't frown or acknowledge it in any way. "I never thought to return, to be honest. There are… painful memories in this town." He placed his empty mug on her coffee table.

Painful memories. Curiosity ate at her. She'd been bouncing around in time while Gray grew up here, but had spent maybe six months in Lobster Cove while Stanley raised Gray and his sister. They'd been teenagers. That had been the only point when Stanley had been unable—or unwilling?—to help her.

Should she ask? Keep her nose out of his business? She knew the polite way to go, but… "So everything isn't always rosy in Lobster Cove?" What a joke. She of all people knew the answer to that one.

He leaped up and Havoc raised his head with a soft, "woof."

She didn't need the dog to tell her Gray wasn't over whatever this town had done to him. She knew the feeling. And she couldn't blame him for not answering her. She'd been pushing it.

And why? She'd never been a big one for gossip. Yet, she had a strange compulsion to know everything she could about Gray. Was it because he was Stanley's nephew? Perhaps. She'd always wondered why Stanley had shut her out during that time. Maybe these painful memories of Gray's had something to do with it.

He stalked across the room. Havoc watched his progress from the comfort of her lap.

"I never planned on returning to Lobster Cove, but circumstances being what they are..."

He sank onto the raised hearth, arms on knees, one hand rubbing the back of his neck. "I don't like to talk about it. Sorry if I come off as rude."

"Not at all."

"We need to discuss the situation here, though."

"The second floor will take quite some time to be rendered habitable." She made a mental list of all the tasks that needed to be completed before he could move in. "It's not just all the clutter." She ticked items off on her fingers. "The bathroom was never completed, the insulation's only half done, all the appliances need to be replaced..." The expression on his face made her stop.

He frowned, his eyes closed. He'd stopped rubbing his neck and moved on to massaging his temples. Fine lines creased around his eyes and at the corners of his mouth. A pang of sympathy struck her. She might have gone over to wrap an arm around his shoulders if Havoc hadn't weighed her down.

Probably for the best.

He straightened and opened his eyes. "Uncle Stan's estate is... tied up at the moment and what little I have access to has gone to pay his hospital bills."

"That's awful."

It's none of your business; stay out of it.

But she really wanted to ask what he meant by *tied up*. It hit her then. Tension flooded her body. Her mouth pursed like she'd been sucking on lemons. She leaned forward. "What about this house?" Havoc slipped off the couch with a reproachful glare. "Can you afford to keep it?"

If he sold it she was in trouble. She'd never bothered signing a lease. Stanley had given her a fantastic deal because of their history and he knew she'd never do anything to let him down. Besides the fact he didn't need the money. "Wait a moment. Why would you need to pay for Stanley's bills? Surely his estate would take care of all that?"

"It should, but a claim's been made on the estate, so it's on hold until everything's settled."

"What? I'm confused. Who would make a claim?" She thought of all the people in Stanley's life. He'd given her the update when she came back to this century. His wife had passed away; he had no children. His nephew was the only relative he ever talked about. There'd been some kind of falling out with the niece. She assumed everything would go to Gray.

"I can't discuss the details. But it will take a while." His knuckles whitened as his hands clenched into fists. "In the meantime, Uncle Stan had me listed as co-owner of this property and the building where you have your store, so they've already passed to me. I just have to deal with a few tax issues."

Uh oh. The dreaded T word. If he couldn't afford the taxes, did that mean she might lose her shop, her home? Just when she finally felt settled.

"A-Are you saying you might have to sell?" She

curled her fist under the fold of Havoc's uncropped ear. Hopefully, the silky flap would hide her tension from Gray. She tried to keep her voice steady and silently cursed her stutter. She didn't want him to know how much this conversation was getting to her.

"It's possible. Your rent barely covers maintenance and taxes."

She stiffened. "I know Stanley was kind to me, but it was all I could manage. He assured me—are you saying he's been carrying me the past few years?" She'd never wanted that. Never. Not for a moment in the past fifteen years had she accepted pure charity. No matter how little she'd had. And she'd almost always started with nothing when she time traveled. Each time the curse took hold, she was left with nothing but what she had on her.

She considered her spell a curse, she'd messed it up so badly. She'd meant to leave the town, instead she'd ended up stuck here forever. Whenever she tried to leave, she ended up at a different point in Lobster Cove history.

Through it all, she'd taken care of herself. Even that first trip through time, she'd worked to survive. Stanley would have helped her more back then, but she wouldn't hear of it and he'd found a job for her at a family friend's restaurant. Hard work, but she'd been used to far worse. And at least she'd done it on her feet rather than flat on her back.

"No, of course not. Uncle Stan was a practical man. No matter how much he liked someone personally, he'd never let that affect his business. He may not have been making a profit, but he wasn't losing."

Should she believe him? Did she have a choice? "Thank you for saying that."

He nodded. "It's the truth. But we still have a problem. I've gotten a good offer on this place. The wisest thing to do is to sell it and be done with it."

She should have known. The minute he came in and told her Stanley was dead, she should have realized he was kicking her out. "How long do I have? I hope you'll at least give me a few months to make alternate arrangements." She remembered the other rentals she'd researched before taking Stanley's offer of this place. She was doomed.

He sighed. "Look. I don't want to sell. And I don't think Uncle Stan would appreciate me kicking you out on your a—behind." He stood.

She craned her neck to keep her gaze on his face when he moved and towered over her. Havoc's tail thumped against the cushions.

"Listen, I just got here. I've been dealing with a lot lately and I'm exhausted. Let's table this for the night and get some rest. Tomorrow I'll reassess the situation and see if we can't figure out a way to keep this place. Okay? Give me some time to figure out how things stand. Good night."

He left before she could come up with a reply.

****

Crap. What was he doing?

He dropped onto the frilly girl comforter with the big roses and stared at the ceiling. He'd dug himself in deep here. What the hell made him tell her he thought of selling? She'd looked at him like he'd run over her dog.

Now he felt like an asshole. He should go out there

and reassure her he wouldn't be kicking her out of her home anytime soon. Or at all. Uncle Stan had wanted her taken care of. He was probably rolling over in his grave after the way Gray had just treated his favorite tenant.

Gray just couldn't shake the story Sherri had fed him. True, Isabeau didn't come off as a "gold-digging bitch" as Sherri had called her. But then again, neither had Lisa when they'd first met.

He'd been fooled once, he wasn't eager to be taken advantage of again.

He swung off the bed and unpacked his bags into the whitewashed armoire with the fancy handles. Jeez, this place was not meant for a man. He should get a pair of needle nose pliers to open the drawer, his fingers were likely to crush the flimsy thing. He wouldn't last long here.

Especially not with her bedroom directly across the hall. Her door had been wide open when he'd stowed his bags and he couldn't help a nice long look before joining her for dinner.

He should have resisted. She wasn't exactly neat, and he'd gotten a good glimpse of some of her underthings strewn across the bed. He fought back an erection just thinking about it. He could picture her in the scrap of lace bra and panties. The deep purple would be sexy as hell against her pale skin.

Damn. He almost hoped she was a slut out for money. Then he could throw some her way and have no qualms when he left after sating his hunger.

He folded his duffle and tucked it away in a corner. As he stowed his other bag, he found the file with Uncle Stan's will inside. He brought it over to the bed and sat. The will hadn't come as a surprise. His uncle had been straightforward about his wishes. Pretty much everything had been left to Gray to manage.

If his sister ever cleaned up her act for real, Gray would happily turn over half the estate to her. He'd had that discussion with his uncle a long time ago, and had every intention of seeing it through even though he was under no legal obligation to do it.

He hoped he'd have the chance. Connie was messed up, but he loved her. If she'd ditch the asshole drug dealer she married, maybe it could happen someday. He wasn't holding his breath.

The only surprise in his uncle's last wishes had come in the form of a small manila envelope. He separated this from the stack of papers and shook it upside down until a handwritten letter and safe deposit key fell out. No one had known anything about it. Well, except for Uncle Stan's secretary. His uncle had been too weak to hold a pen toward the end so she'd written the letter for him. Nancy had considered not passing on the envelope, afraid his uncle's words made him sound insane. She was a sweet lady, who hadn't wanted Gray to think badly of his uncle in his final days.

And the contents *were* crazy.

The words anyway. The sentiment was pure Uncle Stan.

If Isabeau turned out to be whom Uncle Stan thought she was, and not some bitch out to take him for a ride, she'd never have to worry about rent again. Uncle Stan had made it clear he wanted her to have the building, as well as the contents of the safe deposit box this key fit. Gray tossed the key in his palm. He was tempted to go to the bank and see for himself exactly what his uncle had left her. But it wasn't really his business. He tucked the paperwork in a drawer under his clothes.

He'd fully intended to pass Isabeau the envelope right away. But Sherri's words of caution struck him hard. He couldn't stomach the thought that Isabeau had taken advantage of his uncle, much as Lisa had done to him. Of course, he'd also planned on spending a few weeks on the top floor, not holed up in this tiny apartment with a woman who made him realize exactly how long it had been since he'd stopped sleeping with his ex.

Shit. His thoughts had come back full circle.

He heard the shower turn on in the bathroom. The only bathroom. Another issue. How was he supposed to share a bathroom with her? The May nights were still cold, but sweat dripped under his collar. Heat steamed from the vent beside the bed. She must be one of those people who are always cold to have the temp turned so high. He stripped down to his boxers and tossed his rumpled suit over the back of a chair.

He crossed the room to the large window overlooking the side yard. The pane stuck so he struck the frame with the palm of his hand until it gave. A few slivers of chipped paint fluttered to the ground. Cool air washed over his heated flesh.

The water stopped and he imagined Isabeau wrapping herself in one of the thick, blue towels he'd noticed hanging from a hook. It probably didn't even cover the lower globes of her ass.

He had to stop thinking about her or he wouldn't be able to hide his body's reaction. He threw on sweats and a tee. When her bedroom door snicked shut with a soft *thud*, he slipped out, pocketed the master key Uncle Stan had left for him, and headed down the street at a brisk trot.

A hard run would do him good. Get him nice and tired. Maybe then he could stop picturing Isabeau naked and focus on figuring out whether she deserved the windfall his uncle had planned to drop in her lap.

Chapter Four

Isabeau rolled over with a groan. She glanced at her alarm clock through slitted lids. Six a.m. Why in the world was she awake?

Noise filtered through her dreamy haze. Coming from the kitchen? She jerked to a sitting position. The door to her room gaped open. She'd cracked it an inch last night for Havoc. Was the dog making those noises?

She strained to hear, closing her eyes to concentrate. The *click-click* of the burner turning on told her it wasn't Havoc.

Gray? Must be. She'd almost forgotten about Stanley's nephew. Guess he'd taken her at her word to make himself comfortable. Her stomach rumbled at the smell and sound of bacon frying.

Had he gone shopping? She never kept bacon around. Too tempting. Her waistline wouldn't survive having it readily available.

Maybe that's where he'd gone last night?

She'd heard him leave, but not return. She'd been a little upset to realize he must have a key to her place. She should have expected it since Stanley had kept one. But somehow that had never bothered her. Gray having one left her unsettled. And it would have been nice if he'd mentioned it.

She struggled out of bed and grabbed her robe from the floor where she'd dropped it last night. She fingered the flimsy material and thought better of wearing it out of her room. It would barely cover her. Instead, she pulled on a pair of yoga pants and top. Form-fitting, but decent coverage. And she wouldn't look like she'd tried to make herself attractive for him.

Zut alors.

Was that what she was doing? The man might end up kicking her out of her home, and she was worried about whether or not he found her attractive? She ought to have her head examined.

The smell drew her to the kitchen. Maybe he'd left enough bacon so she could cook a few slices for herself.

She came to a quick stop when she reached the doorway. Dressed in sweatpants and a tight tee, Gray hovered over the stove, scooping a massive amount of eggs into one of her covered bowls. Wow, the man had an appetite. There was easily enough for four or five people.

Her gaze strayed to the table. Set for two? She looked back and forth between him and the place settings. Had he actually made breakfast? For her?

"I hope you like bacon and eggs," he said, still facing the stove.

He had. He'd made breakfast for her. She couldn't remember the last time someone had cooked for her. She'd been on her own a long time. She cleared her throat. "Love 'em. Thanks."

Havoc leaned heavily against Gray's leg. Gray's whole body shifted to accommodate the heavy bulk of the dog. Havoc let out a soft whine and rubbed his muzzle against Gray's knee.

"Sorry, dog. No bacon for you."

With one last thump against Gray's leg, Havoc hefted his body up and ambled over to plop his foot on Isabeau's toes.

She grunted in discomfort, but couldn't help but laugh as she patted her dog's enormous head. She was rewarded with one of his pleased groans and a soulful gaze.

"Have a seat. Breakfast is just about ready."

"Let me just take Havoc for a little walk."

"No need. I walked him before I started breakfast." He picked up the bowl of eggs and gestured to the table. "Cold eggs suck. Take a seat."

"O—Okay." Seeing that he hadn't put out anything to serve the eggs with, she grabbed a large spoon out of the drawer and took her place at the table. When he was seated, she lifted the lid and served him a large portion, and a much smaller scoop for herself.

He nodded his thanks and dumped half a pound of bacon on each of their plates. It looked delicious. She bit into one crispy end and let her eyes slip closed in bliss. Perfect.

Gray's low chuckle had her eyes pop back open to find his gaze on her. "I see you weren't lying about loving bacon. I was a little unsure given the other contents of your fridge. Other than the take-out, I'd have thought you were a rabbit with all the veggies you've got in there."

She returned his smile and then tucked into her meal. "When I first came here as a teenager, with ample food available at all times, I admit I overindulged." She patted her now mostly-flat stomach. "And gained quite a few pounds as a result. I've found moderation to be in order." She took another bite and thought of the

Chinese food they'd devoured last night. "Although I can't resist indulging now and then."

He'd paused with his fork halfway to his mouth. He lay it back down without finishing the scoop of eggs.

She glanced at him curiously. What had she said?

"Did you not have enough food as a kid?"

Oh, no. She hadn't meant to reveal so much about herself. Heat rose in her cheeks and she shoveled food into her mouth to buy some time. She waved the fork around and mumbled through a mouthful. "No. Just an all-natural diet. We only ate what was in season and could grow for ourselves." Great, if he understood a word of that, he'd think she was Amish or something. Not that she'd lied. She'd just taken the truth out of context.

She gulped down the rest of the meal and stood. "I have to go through some inventory before I open the store at ten. I better hurry." She quickly rinsed her dishes and laid them in the bottom of the sink. "I'll take care of the dishes later. Make yourself at home." She dashed out of the kitchen and shut herself up in the bathroom without giving Gray a chance to say another word.

****

Gray wasn't buying it. He cast an appreciative glance at the sway of Isabeau's ass as she fled the room before returning his attention to his breakfast.

He'd enjoyed watching her pleasure in the food he'd cooked for her. Lisa had barely eaten a thing in his presence the entire year they'd dated. The only pleasure she'd taken from food was in letting all her friends know how much a meal had cost or who of note had been at the restaurant while they were.

Isabeau had savored every bite. Until the end where she'd made up that ridiculous story about only eating what she grew. He'd already planned on taking a rake to the mess of a garden in the back. The woman was definitely *not* a farmer.

He'd known hunger himself before Uncle Stan took him and Connie in. When their father was in one of his drunken binges, he'd drink the food money. Gray had taken a crappy job at the Lobster Cove Grocery Mart when he was fourteen because Mr. and Mrs. Troy had been willing to give him partial pay in store credit—and ignore the fact he wasn't old enough to work there. They were good people, they knew why he needed that kind of deal. Anytime he'd brought home cash and been stupid enough to let his father catch a glimpse of it, it'd been gone before he could make a shopping list.

Perhaps he and Isabeau had more in common than he'd thought.

And what had she meant about coming here as a teenager? Sherri'd said Isabeau only moved here a few years ago.

Damn.

He had to stop second-guessing everything Isabeau said. She must have meant when she moved to the US, not Lobster Cove specifically. After all, her sexy French accent wasn't from around here.

The questions were adding up and he was eager to get to the bottom of the mystery she presented.

Strictly to satisfy himself she was worthy of the settlement his uncle had intended for her, of course.

He brought his dishes to the sink and made quick

work of cleaning up the mess he'd made preparing breakfast. He hoped she wouldn't expect him to cook for her all the time now. Breakfast was his specialty. For any other meal, his strong suit was knowing where to call for a reservation.

His cell rang. A quick glance at the screen brought an involuntary groan. "What do you want, Lisa?" He tried to keep the exasperation from his voice, but he'd had it with her. She called at least twice a day.

"When are you coming home, darling?" her voice purred over the line. "I miss you."

A few months ago, he'd have come running after hearing that tone in her voice. It meant she'd bought some slinky new negligee and was in the mood to show off. He'd always enjoyed the show. But once he'd realized it was her way of keeping him, and his money, on her hook, the sound had begun having the opposite effect.

"I'm not."

An edge of steel crept into her tone. "If you don't get your ass back here soon, I just may not be here."

"Good!" He laughed. Was she finally taking him seriously?

"Oh, come on, baby." The sexy tone was back. "So we had a little fight. I forgive you. Come home."

"You. Forgive. Me?" He choked out the words. He had to relax his grip on his phone before he crushed it. The urge to throw something clenched in his gut.

She must have sensed his mood had taken a violent turn because a hint of tears entered her voice. "I'm sorry, sweetie. I've missed you so much. Please come home. If you don't come soon, we'll miss the Preston Club gala tomorrow night."

Ah, so that was it. "You're incredible, you know that?"

"Oh, darling. I'm so glad you've come to your senses. Will you be back in time to have dinner at Le Bernardin first?"

Clueless. Completely clueless. "Sarcasm, Lisa. Look it up."

****

Isabeau dusted the shelves as she waited for Logan Price to arrive for their appointment. She glanced at the lobster clock above the door. He'd better get there soon or she'd be closed for the day. She hoped he remembered she closed early on Mondays.

She did not want him seen at her shop after hours. His wife didn't need any more reasons to hate her. Especially when Logan had sworn Isabeau to secrecy about their business together. If his wife confronted Isabeau, she wouldn't be able to explain his presence in her store.

It was like reliving her past. And look how well that had turned out.

Havoc whined and paced, picking up on her tension. Further evidence the dog was her familiar.

When he trotted through the stock room to the back door, she let him out into the fenced-in yard. He grabbed one of his toys and wagged his tail at her.

"Sorry, Havoc. I have some work to do. I'll take you for a nice walk later."

He gazed at her a moment, then turned away to sniff around the grass.

She needed to figure out a place to perform an animal familiar ritual. With Gray at her house, she couldn't do it there. He'd been staying with her for almost a week now and she really needed to find some alone time to focus on her craft. Her rituals were for herself alone. She wasn't prepared to do them with an audience.

She used to meet with the Lobster Cove coven, but they were Wiccan, not witches, so that could get awkward if her magick took on a visual form. The one time that had happened she'd been lucky enough that all the women had closed their eyes in meditation so they hadn't seen her hovering a foot off the ground. Wiccans performed their rituals and believed in their power, but in a much more spiritual than physical sense. Her magick was much more powerful than anything they were used to. After that night, she'd realized she had to go it alone.

The bell above the entrance sounded as the door swept open. She breathed a sigh of relief when Logan burst in.

"Hi, Isabeau. Sorry I'm late. I had to wait for Sherri to take Melanie to soccer." He ran a hand through his thinning reddish-brown hair. He had a large canvas bag slung over his shoulder, stuffed to bursting. "She's not particularly pleased that I left her to do it. I've got to get over to the field in a few minutes so she can head home and get some rest."

"No problem, step on into the back and let's see what you have." She led the way into her storage area, eager to see what he'd brought.

She wasn't disappointed. "These are fantastic. They'll fetch a pretty penny." She trailed her hand over the delicate lines of a nineteenth century perfume vial. Obviously original, but in perfect condition. She bit her lip and studied Logan across the worktable where he'd laid out his assortment of antiques. "Are you sure you want to part with these?"

He nodded. "Yeah. They've been boxed up in the attic for years and I really want to get that bracelet for Sherri."

Isabeau smiled at the light that shone in his eyes when he talked about his wife. Sherri Evard-Price was a lucky woman to have a man so devoted to her. If only she realized it. By all other accounts Sherri was a calm, confident woman. But when it came to Isabeau, she transformed into a raving lunatic.

Isabeau picked up a gilded silver hairbrush and shuddered. It was exactly like the one her childhood best friend had owned. Isabeau had wanted one in the way only a kid living in poverty can truly understand.

To her it had stood for wealth and security. If someone could afford to spend that much on a brush for goodness sake, they had it made. Oh, how she'd envied her friend for all those little luxuries she'd taken for granted while Isabeau struggled to help her mother wash enough clothes so they could eat at least once a day.

Logan plucked it from her grasp. "That shouldn't be here. Sorry about that. This has been passed down in Sherri's family for generations. She wouldn't want to part with it."

Isabeau's stomach churned. Not just a look-a-like then. It really was the actual brush that had caused her so much trouble at Heloise's house on that fateful afternoon in 1692. She stifled the urge to snatch the artifact from Logan's hand and throw it out the window.

Logan gave her a funny look. "You okay?"

She nodded. Sweat beaded on her upper lip. She tasted salt on the tip of her tongue and dabbed at her mouth with her sleeve. "Yes. I'm fine, thank you. Just felt a little dizzy there for a moment."

He pulled her work chair from behind her desk and wheeled it in her direction. "Have a seat then."

She dropped into the chair with a sigh. He squatted next to her, grabbed her wrist and stared at his watch. She rolled her eyes. Why did EMTs feel the need to take everyone's pulse all the time?

He released her wrist with a satisfied grunt. "Strong pulse. A trifle fast, but nothing to worry about. Can I get you some water?"

She patted his hand where it still lay on top of hers. "I'm fine. Really."

The back door swung open. She twisted around to see who would barge in like that.

Gray. She didn't like the expression on his face. He seemed cold. Maybe a bit angry though she couldn't imagine why. Her heart stuttered. Bad news? Was he going to sell her home?

Havoc bounded in after him, a demolished tennis ball clenched in his huge jowls. Ribbons of drool hung from his jaws, dripping onto her floor. She'd have to wipe that up before she slipped on it.

Logan squeezed her hand and stood, his shoulder grazing her breasts as he did. She leaned back in the chair. She hadn't realized they'd been so close.

Gray's face was wiped clear of his cold expression, as if he'd dropped a mask of polite interest over his emotions when Logan approached him with outstretched hand.

She popped out of her seat. "Logan, may I

introduce Grayson Wright? Stanley's nephew. Gray, this is Logan. I was feeling a little faint and Logan helped me to my chair." Why was she babbling? "Logan's an EMT."

Havoc butted his head under her hand and she absentmindedly petted him as the two men sized each other up.

Neither winced as they shook hands, but from the tight grip and whitening of the pinched skin of their fingers, she knew this was no gentle clasping of palms. She snorted. Men.

She grabbed Logan by the shoulders and turned him toward the store. "You should get going. It's almost seven. Don't you have a ball game to get to?"

He jerked as if she'd struck him. "Damn. Yeah, I better get a move on. Thanks, Isabeau. I'll give you a call. Nice to meet you, Grayson." He gave her a friendly peck on the cheek and rushed out the front.

Isabeau turned back to Gray and found him watching Logan's retreating back with narrowed eyes. A shiver of unease skittered up her spine.

****

Gray forced his hands to unclench as Isabeau turned toward him. He had no basis for the irrational anger that had overtaken him when he'd walked in on her and her lover cozying up in the back room of her shop.

She could have a dozen lovers. It was none of his business. Her social life had no bearing on what he was doing here—unless it proved she had been taking advantage of his uncle.

He still didn't like it. He especially didn't like the wedding ring he'd spied on her lover's finger.

Something should be said, but neither of them broke the tense silence. He gritted his teeth.

None of my business. None of my business.

Havoc shoved his snout in his hand. The feeling of cold slime on his skin penetrated his thoughts and he broke eye contact with Isabeau to glare down at the silent dog, who immediately trotted to Isabeau's side and dropped the tennis ball at her feet.

That surprised a laugh out of him and improved his mood immensely.

Isabeau cast him a quizzical glance. "What's so funny?" she asked with a smile.

"I was coming to see if you wanted to get some dinner when I saw Havoc digging a hole in the yard. I figured I'd teach him to play fetch. He spent the entire time chewing that ball into a messed up pile of fuzz and rubber or playing keep-a-way with me." He gestured to the mess at her feet. "So what does he do the minute we come in? Hand the ball over to you. I guess he knows who's boss around here."

She squatted in front of the dog making kissing noises and then rubbing his belly after he flopped onto his back. This left Gray with a clear view straight down her flimsy blouse. A hint of purple tantalized him as he recognized the lacy bra he'd seen on her bed that first night.

He shifted his gaze away before he embarrassed himself.

With one last kiss and pat, she left the dog worshipping at her feet and rose to face him. He was hard pressed to keep his gaze on her face.

"Are you feeling better now?"

Her forehead scrunched and she tilted her head.

"Better?"

He indicated the chair where he'd walked in on her and her *EMT*. "Feeling faint?" The fact he had to remind her didn't bode well for her story.

It took a moment before enlightenment dawned in her expression. "Ah, yes. Much better, thank you kindly."

Because she'd never felt faint to begin with? He wished these doubts didn't keep popping into his brain. He wanted to believe her, but trust didn't come easy lately.

Tension rose in the air as the silence lengthened, the only sound Havoc's heavy panting. Gray searched for something to break the mood. His gaze fell on a pile of junk on a table in the center of the room. "So what's with all the old stuff?"

She shifted from foot to foot as she surveyed the assortment. "Just some new items for the shop. They should probably go to Charlotte at One Enchanted Evening, the consignment shop, but…"

But she'd sweet-talked her lover into letting her have them. He frowned at the pieces as he looked them over. There was something familiar about a few of them. Where had he seen them before?

He shook off the feeling. There were probably dozens of similar items in every antique or pawn shop he'd ever been in. Where else would he have seen such a fancy vase or child-size tea set? His suspicions were overriding his judgment.

"I'm going to walk Havoc home and organize all this tomorrow." She grabbed a white sheet from under the worktable and flicked it open over the pile. "Give me a second to close up the shop." She disappeared into the store for a minute. When she returned she flipped a bunch of switches and the display areas went dark. "Keep the front room lights out or someone's bound to want to shop around." She rolled her eyes. "It never fails. I can go hours without a single customer, but the second I flip the lock, someone's at the door, dying to come in."

He chuckled. "Works the same at the office. The minute I shut down my computer, someone calls with an emergency that must be handled right then. Never mind if it's seven o'clock on a Friday night and I've been at my desk since dawn."

"Long hours—almost as long as retail." She smiled. "Stanley mentioned you own your own business. I guess it's the price we pay for working for ourselves. If we don't work, we don't get paid." She clicked Havoc's leash on his collar and shrugged. "I don't mind though. I love my shop and *mostly* enjoy my customers. Even when they come in late."

She gave him a jaunty little wave and sashayed out the back door, Havoc trotting at her side.

Chapter Five

Havoc walked peacefully alongside Isabeau. She kept a good grip on his leash, just in case, but he didn't make any effort to pull away.

A squirrel ran directly in front of them and up a birch tree that lined the sidewalk. Havoc watched its antics intently, but made no move to give chase.

She patted him on the head. "Good boy, Havoc."

Main Street flowed out before her. The bay off to her left, the park to her right. Many of the shops bustled with activity as the streetlights switched on and the sky darkened steadily. People crowded the restaurants. Outside seating appeared to be at a premium on such a gorgeous night. Several places kept white Christmas lights on their trees year-round. They twinkled to life and lent a magical air to the town.

She inhaled a long breath of the crisp, clean night air. Her favorite time of day. People stared at her and Havoc, either crossing the street to get away from the enormous dog, or doing the exact opposite. Progress was slow as she let Havoc soak up the attention.

Truth be told, she liked the attention herself. Normal, everyday type of attention. Almost immediately upon setting herself up in town, she'd gained the reputation of being a witch. People might have ignored the ravings of the person who'd seen her arrive in this time—who would believe Isabeau had appeared out of thin air?—but she'd made the mistake of buying her conjuring supplies in town rather than ordering online. One too many black candles and strange herbs, combined with Sherri's knack for spreading rumors, and people started whispering "witch" behind her back. Ridiculous in this day and age, but there it was. Along with the reputation came the snide remarks and sideways glances. But not tonight with people's attention on Havoc rather than herself.

Footsteps on the pavement behind her caused her heart to jump. Havoc gave her a reassuring bump with his nose, his energy assuring her no one was out to do her any harm. Her pulse continued to race, just not from fear.

A part of her had hoped he'd follow. She tossed a glance over her shoulder to confirm it was him and slowed.

It didn't take him long to catch up. "It's a nice night. I figured I'd join you. I've been holed up in the attic too long."

"It is a dreadful mess up there. I'm afraid dear Stanley was a bit of a pack rat."

Gray laughed. "That's putting it mildly. I just unearthed an entire box of magazines from the sixties. I don't want to know what's in some of the others."

A chill ran down her arms, raising uncomfortable gooseflesh up and down her body. Stanley kept mementos from the sixties? She'd been caught in any number of photographs back then. The idea of capturing her image on film had been terrifying at first—would they capture her soul as well?—But once she got over her irrational fear, she'd taken every opportunity to see the phenomenon for herself. Plus, the media of the time thought she had the perfect look to represent the era. Had Stanley saved those photos? What would Gray think if he came upon such evidence of Isabeau's past?

"Really? How interesting." Did she sound as flummoxed as she felt? "Perhaps there would be something of interest for the historical society. I would love to go through them, if that's permissible?"

"I was thinking of renting a dumpster and making a clean break of it, but if you think there might be something of value, feel free to take a look."

"That is most kind of you." Good. This would give her a chance to find anything that could reveal her true history. "I should have realized what an enormous task you have undertaken. Would you like some assistance?"

"What about your store? Don't you need to be there to take care of your customers?"

She shrugged. "I have several employees who oversee the shop for me on occasion. My customers will be well taken care of, I assure you." Havoc nudged her closer to Gray, so she put a hand on his arm. "I would be pleased to help you in any way I can. I know this is a difficult time for you."

He studied her for a second, then covered her hand with his and nodded. "I'd like that. Thanks."

Someone made to brush by them but didn't get more than a step past before turning with a huge smile. Isabeau stifled her groan. Nina Carson was the town gossip. Within hours, she'd have the whole town convinced the local witch had somehow bewitched the returning prodigal son.

Merde.

"Grayson Wright, as I live and breathe!" She held out her arms to Gray as if expecting him to run into her embrace.

Isabeau tried not to smirk as he merely regarded the invitation with a raised eyebrow.

When he failed to respond as Mrs. Carson wished, she resorted to grabbing and holding him at arms' length to look him up and down. "You've certainly grown into those lanky legs of yours now, haven't you? You were all skin and bones last I saw you." Her expression turned sorrowful, but she couldn't hide the sparkle in her eyes. "I was so sad to hear of your uncle. Such a sweet man, he was. Oh, how he would have enjoyed having you back here in town. I must say we all despaired of ever seeing you again. And to think today I see not one, but two, Wright children. If only it were under better circumstances."

Two Wright children? Gray's sister was in Lobster Cove? Isabeau noted the almost blissful smile on Mrs. Carson's face as she watched Gray. Interesting news, yes, but did it really deserve such unalloyed glee? Mrs. Carson only ever got that excited over murder and mayhem, not a mere family visitation.

Havoc growled low and Mrs. Carson took a hasty step back, eyeing the dog warily. "Well, then. I'm afraid I must be off. So good to see you Grayson." She gave a stiff nod at Isabeau. "Miss Munier. A pleasant day to you."

"Have a good evening, Mrs. Carson." Isabeau kept the polite smile on her face until the old bat had turned completely away and proceeded to cross the street.

Isabeau shuddered. It was eerie how similar some of the present day people were to those of the past. Mrs.

Carson was the spitting image of Madame Talbert—the preacher's wife who'd spread the news Isabeau was a witch so fast Isabeau was convicted before she'd had any chance to defend herself.

Mrs. Carson had done the same within moments of meeting Isabeau three years ago. Granted, she had good reason to run around hysterically claiming Isabeau a witch. Seeing a person materialize out of thin air didn't happen every day. Just Isabeau's luck the town gossip witnessed her arrival in this time.

With a muttered apology, Gray whirled around and strode off in the opposite direction. Havoc took off after him, forcing Isabeau to run to catch up. She'd been so caught up in her memories, she'd forgotten all about Gray for a moment.

"Gray, wait!" She grasped Havoc's leash in a death grip, stumbling along in the giant's wake and praying to keep her legs under her. At this pace, she'd end up with more than a few scrapes and bruises if she tripped. Not to mention, Havoc's determination to stay with Gray. If she fell, would her dog drag her along?

Thankfully, Gray must have heard her gasping plea because he glanced over his shoulder and came to a slow stop. Havoc careened around his legs, crashing her against Gray's chest. He dropped his hands to her waist to steady her.

She would have cursed Havoc for putting her in such a situation. But she liked it too much.

****

Gray wrapped his hands around Isabeau's waist, the flimsy fabric of her blouse soft against his palms, the heat from her body soaking through to warm him. She felt good pressed up against him like this.

He shook himself out of the stupor her proximity caused. She smelled like oranges and he had the strong desire to find out if she tasted of them as well.

Havoc's leash dug into the backs of his knees, pulled tight as the dog circled them then plopped down to rest against the backs of her legs. If he didn't know any better he'd say the dog was playing matchmaker.

Isabeau's hands curled into fists against his stomach. Her chest rose rapidly as she caught her breath. "I'm so sorry. I don't know what came over him."

"That's all right." He reluctantly grabbed the leash, unwinding them and taking a step back. A little breathing room was definitely in order.

Her scent lingered. Lotion or perfume? Or had she simply had a piece of fruit with her lunch? Either way, he had to give her credit, the tantalizing smell did much more for him than any of the nauseating flower perfumes Lisa doused herself with.

Damn, but he had to get his head on straight. Lisa had worked a number on him, that was for sure. He couldn't tell the difference between seduction and innocence any more. One day soon he had to decide whether Isabeau was the temptress Sherri had made her out to be, or if he could trust his instincts and believe she was as sweetly innocent as he hoped.

"Are you okay?"

"What?" He looked down at himself but couldn't see any reason for her question. "I'm fine. The dog's a powerhouse, but he took it relatively easy on me."

She shook her head. "That's not what I meant. You seemed distraught after speaking with Mrs. Carson."

All thoughts of oranges and seduction fled his

mind. "That old—" He cringed at the thought of the nosy old woman. "She's just like I remember. Loves to gossip and stir up trouble." He studied Isabeau's face a moment and didn't notice any of the avarice he'd spied on Mrs. Carson's. A small leap of faith then. Hopefully it wouldn't bite him in the ass later. "I'm fine. I just wasn't expecting my sister to show up in Lobster Cove."

Havoc let out a small whine, so Isabeau gave him a gentle pat. She took hold of his leash and gestured down the street with an inquiring gaze.

He nodded and they turned down Birch Avenue toward her house.

"Stanley never said much about her to me. Just that she had some problems and they didn't speak any more. I understand if you don't want to talk about it. Please forgive my intrusion."

"Nothing to forgive." He gathered his thoughts as she opened the front door to her home and he followed her in. Havoc bounded over to the armchair and plopped down, leaving only the couch. He settled into a corner while Isabeau tucked her legs under her on the opposite side. "Connie's an alcoholic and drug addict. Has been for a long time. Ever since our brother died when we were young. I used to try to help her, but…" He shrugged. How to explain the years he'd spent tormenting himself over his sister? How the guilt sometimes ate him up inside and the worry kept him awake at night? "I hadn't seen her in over a year. She married her dealer and basically disappeared. Then when Uncle Stan died, her husband decided they were in for a windfall. He was less than pleased when he learned Uncle Stan left everything to me." He ran a hand through his hair, mentally replaying the ugly scene at the lawyer's office in his mind.

Her slim hand covered his with surprising strength. He forced his gaze to remain on her expressive blue eyes as she leaned forward in an offer of comfort. The quick glimpse down her shirt distracted him and caused a tightening in his groin he hoped wasn't obvious.

"That must have been horrible. Stanley would have been displeased to have such a commotion on his behalf. He was never fond of conflict, though I never knew him to run from a fight he thought worth championing."

That surprised a laugh out of him. "He certainly never minded speaking up in front of me, that's for sure." She'd summed up Uncle Stan perfectly. Their connection was so much more than landlord to tenant. The thought was killing him. A surge of anger at his uncle slammed into him.

Whoa. Where had that come from? He'd almost think he was jealous. Ridiculous.

Wasn't it?

"I didn't realize my uncle spent so much time in Lobster Cove the past few years. Ever since Aunt Aggie died and he moved into that over 55 village, I thought he'd become something of a homebody."

She returned to her corner. He regretted the loss of her warm hand on his. Had she touched his uncle in a similar manner? Consoled him over the loss of his beloved wife? Offered a return to youth with the use of her luscious body? He shook away the image that thought brought to mind.

"He'd come see me at least once a month to collect the rent." She twisted her hair around a finger, her gaze

Emma Kaye

fixed on an empty spot on the mantel.

He frowned. Something was odd there. Pictures and knick-knacks cluttered every inch of space above the fireplace except for that one spot. Just the size for a three by five photo frame. Kind of like the one he'd seen her stow in a drawer his first night here.

"I would have liked to visit him as well, but it was too far from town."

"I'd think it would barely take half an hour on that bike you have under the tarp outside. Unless you don't actually ride?"

She jerked up straight like she'd been insulted. "Of course, I ride!" she burst out. "I—I just meant it was difficult to find time away from my store. And I wasn't aware he was in anything other than the perfect health he always appeared to enjoy."

He grabbed her arm when she would have jumped up. "I'm sorry." For thinking the bike was no more than a prop to gain his interest? Had his uncle told her Gray used to ride? It was a trick worthy of his ex. He'd been floored when he learned how much research Lisa had done on him before their "chance" meeting.

He couldn't tell Isabeau that. Why? Because he didn't want her to know his suspicions? Or because he didn't want her to be mad at him? Shit. He feared it was the latter. Not good. "It's just that I've been here over a week now and I haven't seen you take it out even once. I figured you were keeping it for a friend or something."

She eyed him for a moment before she relaxed beside him. "I suppose that is a reasonable assumption. But, no. A motorcycle was my first motorized vehicle upon…" she trailed off, a confused look upon her face.

60

"I don't travel far from home so I've never learned to drive a car."

"You're kidding. What do you do in the winter around here? You can't go anywhere on a bike in a snowstorm."

"I stay home."

One point against his theory. "I love to travel." If she had researched him, she'd know he spent much of the year traveling the country, so saying she liked to stay home would be a turn off for him. Of course, with a woman like her at home, maybe he'd be tempted to stay put more often.

****

That weekend, Isabeau finally got the chance to go for a ride. She reveled in the freedom. The bike hummed beneath her. The miles flew by. Maneuvering the bike took all of her concentration and her cares took a backseat.

She drove aimlessly for a while, not really caring where she ended up. Provided she didn't cross the county line, she was okay. But, oh, how she wished she could travel beyond the boundaries of her island. She loved it here, but there was so much in the world she'd never have the chance to see. The thought drove her crazy.

Almost as much as Gray. She'd seen some of his vulnerable side the other day when he learned his sister was in town. He'd surprised her when he opened up and talked about it, however briefly. Stanley had told her what a private person Gray was, and everything about him since he'd moved into her spare room had confirmed that.

Yet, he'd taken the time to tell her what had

bothered him. He'd opened up to her. She wanted to take some of his burdens from his shoulders. He'd been staying with her for almost two weeks now. During the day, and even into the night, he spent the majority of his time on conference calls for his work. But she'd heard a fair share of his conversations with his lawyer as well. She hadn't tried to eavesdrop—not *really*—but her home didn't allow for a whole lot of personal space. And she'd discovered sound traveled easily through her paper-thin walls.

At least he seemed confident everything would work out. But going through the turmoil of dealing with his sister put a strain on him, that much was obvious. He'd been so tired this morning, her heart ached for him.

She couldn't help directly, but today she hoped to ease his burden as much as it was in her power to do. Nothing direct, that would be unethical without his consent, but maybe she could send a little positive energy his way.

With that thought in mind, she took the winding road up Cadillac Mountain. Part exhilaration, part fear swept her up the dizzying path. She kept her attention ahead of her—sometimes cars coming down spent more time watching the gorgeous views than the road. She kept her eyes off the view completely. The steep drop off threatened to make her ill. Funny that she wasn't fond of heights, and yet, she liked to ride to the peak of the highest point on Mount Desert Island for many of her spells. Like the ride to and from, the extreme reactions of peace and fear the spot provoked balanced her emotions when she took the time to meditate there.

She reached the parking area and put the Savage up

on its kickstand. The lot was crowded, as usual. The mountain's beauty was a big pull for tourists. Still, she found a relatively quiet spot out on the rocks, away from the main thoroughfare. No one ever questioned all the tourists who stepped off the path to wander away from the masses.

Her backpack slid to the ground with a soft *thump*. She hadn't packed much in the way of supplies other than water. A candle would never stay lit with the steady breeze. Besides which, people might give her a few strange looks if she had her full setup. And she preferred to stay out of the spotlight while casting even the smallest of spells.

Thankfully, she'd remembered to bring a blanket to soften the hard rocks. She needed to bring her thoughts under control before she cast her spell and that took time under the best of circumstances. And now, with her thoughts all jumbled because of Gray...

Best to get started and stop worrying. After placing the blanket in the perfect spot, she walked a clockwise circle around it in the guise of straightening the soft tartan fabric. She settled herself as comfortably as possible and cast her gaze out over the mountain, toward Southwest Harbor. The gorgeous rolling hills, with the pine trees in the foreground and the water in the back, helped bring the sense of peace she needed to clear her head.

The wind brought with it the scent of salt water and pine. She breathed deep, enjoying the sensation. Her hair tangled around her shoulders, the strands lightly caressing her face. The wind was just cool enough to keep the sun's strong rays bearable.

Still, sweat trickled down the back of her neck. She

lifted her hair and the breeze cooled the moisture, causing a shiver to run up her spine. Her hands flat against the stone on either side of the blanket, she closed her eyes and concentrated on Gray.

"I wish him peace,
I wish him well.
May all good things
Come with this spell."

She repeated this mantra nine times. Once the power had built sufficiently, she released it into the wind. For a moment, the air swirled wildly around her—she felt like Dorothy caught in that tornado—but soon enough, all was calm again and the breeze just a gentle caress on her cheeks.

To her surprise, the lights of Southwest Harbor had twinkled into existence while she worked her magick. She hadn't realized she'd been there that long. She took a moment to appreciate the view. Sitting on the rocks, far enough from the edge she didn't have to see the drop, she could relax enough to enjoy the sight. This was her favorite time of day up here on the mountain. The whole world was calm and peaceful with a beauty that took her breath away.

She reflected on the spell she'd cast for Gray's benefit. Would it help? She followed the flow of magick around her and felt sure it would. He'd never know what she'd hoped to do for him, but she hoped he was able to reap the benefits.

His well-being had become important to her. Her house no longer felt empty. There was new life within. The vibrations of her home were happy now, rather than merely content as they'd been when she'd been on her own. First Havoc, then Gray. She hadn't realized how much she needed such connections until now.

Walking counter-clockwise around the blanket undid her magick circle and released the last of the pent up energy from her spell.

Isabeau fought a huge yawn as she repacked her backpack. She'd depleted all her energy with that casting. She'd have to be extra careful not to fall asleep on the ride home.

One nagging thought kept her from total exhaustion. If her spell was successful, and Gray's troubles worked themselves out, how long would he stay in Lobster Cove? Had she just chased away the man who had made her house more of a home than she'd ever known?

Chapter Six

Gray let the car idle outside the dilapidated house on Fifth Street. He'd never thought to return here. Never wanted to. But where else would Connie and her scumbag husband have gone? They didn't like to waste money on anything other than the drugs that kept them high as a kite twenty-four seven.

Time hadn't done the place any favors. Their father had left the house entirely to Connie. When Gray didn't attempt to return home after Uncle Stan was awarded custody of him and Connie, Gray's father had disowned him. Connie had snuck back on occasion to make sure the old man had enough to eat, was still alive. Gray hadn't cared.

Despite owning the property, Connie and her husband had never lived there. They'd rented the piece of crap, making enough money to pay the taxes and give them a little extra drug money. How they'd managed to find renters was beyond him. Probably sent fake pictures to fool them into thinking it was some sort of paradise. He felt bad for the poor fools that fell for it.

But at least they didn't have the memories that went along with the house. He clenched and unclenched his fists as he stared at the broken railing on the right half of the porch. His father had sent him through it when he was thirteen. He couldn't remember why. Something to do with his attitude, according to his father. He was pretty sure it had more to do with the fifth of scotch his father had consumed after dinner.

Gray rubbed his left side. His father had broken two of Gray's ribs and his left arm that night, then claimed Gray had fallen off the roof while cleaning the gutters and grounded him for being clumsy.

Bastard.

If only Uncle Stan had taken them all away that night. Connie might never have gotten into the drugs and Brad... maybe Brad would still be alive. He forced himself to continue breathing though the memories threatened to squeeze the air out of his lungs.

The rusty hinges on the screen door squealed as the door slammed against the side of the house. Connie burst through the door, Frank storming after her.

"Leave me alone," she yelled, turning slightly to glare at Frank over her shoulder.

Frank caught up to her, grabbed her upper arm and swung her around to face him. His mottled face twisted in a sneer, he raised his fist and knocked Connie to the ground.

Gray leaped out of the car. He ran to the couple, grabbed Frank's wrist and yanked him around. Once they were face-to-face, he let fly with a jab to Frank's chin followed by a left hook. Frank ended in the dirt next to his wife.

Connie gawked at him like he'd sprouted horns. He held out his hand and waited to see if she'd accept his help.

She stared at his outstretched hand until he thought of withdrawing, but a second later, she reached out to him. With a nod of acceptance, he helped her to her feet.

"What the hell are you doing here?" she asked.

Frank made a move to get up, so Gray pointed at him. "Stay down. I'll deal with you in a minute." Coward that he was, Frank stayed still, though he spat at Gray's feet. The man was beneath his notice, except for the number he'd done on Connie.

"I heard you were in town and came to talk. Why the hell are you still with this guy?"

She tossed her hair back and glanced down at her husband with a sneer. "Not any more. I kicked his ass out after he pulled that shit at Uncle Stan's funeral. He's just not taking no for an answer." She tried to kick at Frank's legs, but Gray pulled her away.

"Stop that."

Frank glared at her as he struggled to his feet. "We ain't over. You're my wife and I'll be damned if you think you can leave me just when you're finally about to bring me some damn money. If I'd known your uncle was such a tightwad, I'd never have married you. No way I'm cutting you loose now."

Gray snorted. He couldn't believe what he was hearing. But maybe he should. He'd always wondered why Frank had made it legal with Connie. He wasn't exactly the marrying type. He should have known.

"You're the reason he cut me out of the will in the first place, asshole." She crossed her arms over her chest. Her hands trembled.

Gray cringed.

When had she had her last fix?

Her breathing was rapid, her face pale. He recognized the signs all too well. She'd come scrambling to him enough times when she'd run out of drug money.

"Enough." He pointed at Frank. "Get the hell out of here. I see you again, you're getting a hell of a lot more than a sore jaw. Got me?" No use threatening with the police. Frank knew how to walk the line in front of the cops. This wasn't the first time he'd raised a hand to Connie.

Frank jumped into his beat-up old sports car. "This ain't over, bitch! I'm gonna get what's comin' to me," he yelled out the window as he drove away.

"You okay?" Gray turned his attention back to Connie. She shook worse than ever.

She jerked her head in a semblance of a nod. "Yeah, yeah. I'm good. Just a little worn out." She pointed to the porch. "I need to sit."

He helped her over to the porch and eased her onto the top step. She leaned against the handrail and closed her eyes.

He kept silent and watched the occasional car pass by. There was so much to say but he had no idea how to bring any of it up. Was there even any point? They'd been through it all before. Did the fact that she'd ditched her dealer husband make any difference? He hoped so.

"I still miss him, you know," she whispered.

He raised his brow. "Frank? You'll be lucky if you don't see him again."

She shook her head. "No. Brad."

A vice pressed against his heart. "Me, too."

She stood and walked into his arms. He almost stopped breathing, but pulled her close. He couldn't remember the last time they'd shared a moment like this. She was usually too busy searching for her next high and he was too busy trying to get her into rehab.

They'd never even talked about Brad's death and the hole he'd left in their lives.

"I'm seeing someone," she mumbled against his chest.

"Already? That's kind of fast, isn't it? Or were you seeing him before you left Frank?"

She giggled and stepped back. "That's not what I meant. I'm seeing a therapist. Sometimes, he actually has me believing Brad's death wasn't my fault."

Tears stung his eyes. "It wasn't. Dad killed him. Not you." And the bastard walked away with barely a scratch, while Brad never breathed again. He'd even managed to convince the judge Brad had been driving when they hit that pole, so he escaped jail time, too. Gray slowly unclenched his fists. He resisted the urge to punch more holes in the dilapidated porch. Experience told him he'd end up with bruised knuckles and the dead feeling still eating away at his gut.

"And I started AA." She swiped at the tears leaving trail marks down her cheeks.

He didn't know what to say. He'd heard it before, but she seemed somehow more…sincere, this time. And she'd finally stood up to Frank. She'd never dared before—she hadn't wanted to upset him. Her asshole husband might have cut off her drug supply and that had always been too great a risk.

He didn't want to think it, but his skeptical side couldn't help but wonder if her sudden desire to get sober had something to do with Uncle Stan's will. "Why now?"

She slapped his shoulder. "Nice. Thanks a lot." Her grin faded. "I guess I deserve that." Her gaze glued to the stairs, she picked at the peeling paint. "I don't know, really. When I got the call that Uncle Stan had died...and I hadn't spoken to him in..." She choked up and tears clouded her eyes once more. "I guess I realized that I hadn't just lost him, I'd thrown him away. And Frank practically cheered because he thought we—really that he—would get a big chunk of money. I looked around at my crappy life and couldn't do it anymore."

"Then I'm glad you're getting some help finally." He nudged her shoulder. "All I've ever wanted was for you to be happy."

"I know. I'm trying." She leaned against him, resting her head on his shoulder.

"And I'll be here to help any way I can."

****

A few days after she performed her spell, Isabeau poked her head through the open door to the second floor apartment. She'd been listening to Gray move boxes around for the past half hour. She didn't want to appear too eager, but she didn't want him unearthing anything suspicious before she got up there.

She spotted him hefting a heavy box from the top of one pile to a space he had cleared out near the window. An assortment of junk cluttered an old oak table pushed up against the wall. Another collection of boxes and piles of paper were neatly stacked on the opposite side of the room. He dropped the box on one end of the table and took a seat in a spindle-legged stool.

"Hello, Gray. May I come in?" she asked quickly before he had the chance to dig in to the overstuffed box.

He shifted toward her voice. She quelled the quick

jump of her heart when he turned those sweet eyes her way. This was the first time she'd seen him with his glasses off, other than when he had his head bent to wipe them clean.

"Hey, there. Please tell me you've come to magically make all of this go away?" He waved his hand toward the mountains of clutter surrounding him.

She laughed. "Sorry, no. The most I can do is provide an extra pair of hands." She rolled up the sleeves of her sweatshirt. "Oh my. It's quite a bit hotter up here than downstairs."

He wiped his arm across his forehead. "Heat rises. You've probably been paying to heat this floor without even realizing it. Once I get this mess taken care of, I'll have someone in to see about fixing that."

"I do appreciate my furnace, so much more efficient than a wood-burning stove." She shivered just thinking about the sorry excuse for a fire she'd shared with her mother once upon a time. Lobster Cove winters could be harsh.

Gray's head tilted to the side as he regarded her. "You keep dropping these little tidbits about your childhood. Makes me wonder if we have more in common than we'd think at first glance."

She frowned as she thought through what she'd said. Oh. The stove comment. Why couldn't she keep her mouth shut around Gray? She never let these little things slip. In all the years she'd been flitting about through time, the only person she'd ever divulged the truth to had been Stan. If he hadn't found her immediately upon her first jump, she never would have said anything to him either.

Now, her loose tongue was determined to give her

away.

"Why don't I start with these boxes while you take care of those bigger items?" She pointed to a dusty corner where an ancient television, a few broken chairs and other odds and ends had been stacked in a muddle.

"Subject change, got it." He rose from his chair and with a sweeping gesture, indicated she should take his seat. "Anything that might have some historical significance, I've piled in that corner over there."

Her cheeks burned with the knowledge he'd seen through her flimsy attempt to avoid deeper conversation, but a part of her melted that he'd give in so easily. Sweet of him not to embarrass her by attempting to find out the juicy details of her past. "Thanks. I'll get started."

They worked steadily for an hour listening to an eclectic mix of songs off Gray's iPod. Isabeau only found one item worthy of the historical society, and nothing that could give away her secret, thank goodness.

Gray's stomach announced lunchtime with a loud rumble she could hear from clear across the room. "Okay. Guess it's about time to stop for lunch. Want to run over to Mariner's Fish Fry and grab something? I could use a little time away from here." He clapped his hands against his legs, sending dust flying around him. He coughed and tried to clear the air with a wave.

"Sounds lovely." She chuckled at the state of her own clothes. Dirt streaked her sweatshirt and jeans. Her hands were disgusting. She couldn't possibly go anywhere looking like this. "I best clean up a bit first."

"Yeah, me too." His eyes sparkled with amusement. "We're a sight, huh?" He picked up a milk crate full of miscellaneous garbage. "You go first. I'll just take a few things out to the dumpster."

She nodded and left. She hadn't been sure they needed a dumpster, but after all the stuff Gray had hauled out of here this morning, she couldn't deny its usefulness any longer.

They'd have to get rid of it pretty quick though. Her neighbors would be upset with her if she left it in her driveway for too long.

With Gray tromping up and down the stairs to the dumpster, she dropped her dirty clothes in the hamper in her room and dashed across the hall to jump in the shower.

She cursed herself when she finished. She'd forgotten to bring clean clothes in with her as she'd gotten used to doing since Gray's arrival. She toweled off and wrapped herself as much as possible. She didn't have far to go. And she'd been quick. Gray was probably still hauling boxes and wouldn't be in the apartment to see her scamper across the hall anyway. So who cared if the towel barely covered her?

The living room was just visible when she inched the bathroom door open to peek out. Darn. Gray had finished his tasks for the morning and stood by the couch, his back to her.

She eased the door open until she could slip through the crack. Just as she was about to run across the hall, Gray shifted and she caught sight of what he held in his hands.

Her hands shook violently where she clutched her wet towel to her chest. She must have made some sound because Gray swiveled in place to face her. Astonishment blazed across his handsome face.

She couldn't blame him. He held a picture of her hugging his uncle—his twenty-four-year-old uncle.

****

Gray stared at Isabeau. He almost forgot the photo he held while watching water trail down her neck from the wild, wet hair clinging to her cheeks and shoulders. Tempting as it was to follow the path of water down to the skimpy towel and further to linger on the long expanse of naked leg below, he forced his gaze to remain above the neck. He already suffered a full-blooded reaction to her nakedness. Obvious enough that he was thankful he hadn't turned completely in her direction when he heard her gasp.

The panicked expression on her face brought his thoughts back to the photo. He'd recognized his uncle immediately. He was in his early twenties—right about the time he'd met and fallen in love with Aunt Aggie. Gray had put a photo from their first date in the coffin with his uncle. The image of him at twenty-five was fresh in his brain.

But who the hell was Uncle Stan with? The woman looked remarkably like Isabeau. Younger. Probably a teenager. Younger than Uncle Stan anyway, but she'd be a hell of a lot older than Isabeau was now.

"Who is this?" He held the photo out toward her. Her mother?

"You wouldn't believe me if I told you."

What kind of a crap answer is that?

"Listen, Isabeau." He whipped off his glasses and pinched the bridge of his nose. "I don't like games. What the hell is going on? I thought you only met my uncle a few years ago, but obviously he knew your mother. What are you hiding? And why?"

Silence met his demand. He shoved his glasses back on so he could see her properly. But she wasn't there. The little... If she thought he'd give up that easy... He stormed down the hall and shoved open her bedroom door.

And stopped dead in his tracks.

Shit.

He should have realized she'd want to put on some clothes.

Thankfully, or unfortunately depending on how he viewed it, she had her back to him. The lacy pink strap of her bra could be snapped open with a quick flick of his fingers. Her arms paused above her head, then quickly yanked a sweatshirt down over her body.

White panties barely covered her tight, sweet ass. She only stood a foot or so inside the door. He could be right up behind her in less than a second.

He whirled around and fled before he gave in to the impulse. He was not the kind of man to accost a woman in her bedroom. He wasn't his father.

He paced the length of her living room as he waited for her to quit hiding. He could only hope she'd take long enough for him to forget what the long lines of her legs and back looked like with the sun shining on her through the curtains.

He snorted. Fat chance. She couldn't possibly stay in her room that long. He wasn't likely to ever banish that image from his mind. If he were honest with himself, he didn't want to. The picture was just too good.

Pictures. He grabbed up the photo of Isabeau's mom and Uncle Stan. Curiosity ate at him. Why didn't she want him to know about the connection? Was she ashamed?

A thought nibbled at the back of his brain. He tried to push it aside, but the thought didn't want to go away now that it had occurred to him. Had his uncle been unfaithful to Aunt Aggie? The girl in the picture was too young, the uncle he knew would never have taken advantage of a young girl like that. But maybe that wasn't the only time they'd met. Had she returned as a young woman and seduced his uncle? Maybe gotten pregnant?

Wild conjecture. All of it. What the hell was he thinking? His uncle never would have cheated on his wife. They'd been the perfect couple.

Which still begged the question of what made Isabeau want to hide the fact her mother knew Uncle Stan?

The floor creaked and he spun to see Isabeau slip into the room. A blush stained her cheeks and she kept her eyes averted to avoid his gaze.

"May I have my picture back, please?"

The soft, fearful note in her voice made him wince. He'd scared her. He clenched his hand around the photo. The smooth glass was cool to his touch, the wooden frame's straight edge dug into his palm. He relaxed his grip and handed the photo over.

She snatched it up and took a step back. Out of range. Did she think he'd hit her? The thought made his skin crawl. He sank onto the sofa. "I'm sorry I barged into your room. I wasn't thinking."

"I accept your apology. I'm sorry I haven't been completely honest about my relationship with your uncle." She sat on a chair facing him. "It's not entirely your business, though."

He straightened.

Not his business?

"He's my uncle."

"And how does that make any of this *your* business?"

"Because—" He cut himself off. She was right. It was none of his business. But damn if he didn't really want to know.

Chapter Seven

An hour later, Isabeau tried to ignore the pleasant weight of Gray's hand at the small of her back. The touch was distracting, to say the least. If she didn't pay attention, she'd trip on the stairs leading up to Mariner's Fish Fry and fall flat on her face.

"Inside or out?"

She blinked. She'd been so preoccupied with his hand, she hadn't noticed they'd entered the restaurant. "Sorry?"

His smile made her blush. He'd obviously noticed her inattention. Did he realize the cause?

"Do you want to get a table inside or out on the deck?"

"Outside, definitely." The deck at Mariner's was one of her favorite spots to eat.

They followed Katelyn Sullivan, the owner's daughter, out back to a cozy spot against the rail. Since they'd come specifically for their famous lobster rolls, Katelyn took their orders and was away in a flash.

"This is nice." Isabeau soaked up the atmosphere. The twinkling Christmas lights added a magical glow. A slight breeze off the bay caressed her face. "Stanley brought me here when I first got into town. I've been coming back ever since. Their blueberry pie, *c'est magnifique*."

"We used to come here too when I was in high

school. Did you and Uncle Stan go out often?" Gray's voice sounded stiff.

Even before he'd found the picture, she'd sensed he didn't like talking to her about Stanley. Each time they did, he acted strange. She couldn't imagine why.

"He was always very kind to me. I owe him more than I can say. Your uncle was a very special man."

He nodded. "I agree."

"He talked of you often. You're lucky you never came to visit. He was determined to set us up. I hope it doesn't embarrass you to know he sang your praises every chance he had. He was very proud of you."

Was that a blush?

"He was like a father to me. Far better than my own ever was. Did he tell you he took me in when I was sixteen?"

"Yes. He wished you were his own son. That he could have raised you and your sister from when you were babies."

A suspicious glint of moisture shown in Gray's eyes. She could have imagined it, the moment was gone so quick—but she didn't think so.

"Him and me, both."

"He cherished the time he *did* have. He only mentioned your sister a few times. I think his inability to help her with her difficulties saddened him." Why the sudden urge to talk about Stanley when the topic was so obviously painful for him? She hoped he wanted to open up to her again, like he had the other day with regards to his sister. Since he'd found the picture of her and Stanley, the air between them had been filled with tension. The strain had begun to wear on her.

Gray leaned back in his chair to let the waitress

place their orders on the table.

The delicious aroma of lobster drenched in butter made her stomach growl. She could only hope he hadn't heard. She took a hearty bite, closing her eyes in bliss. "Oh my, this is delicious."

She smiled at his answering grunt. He devoured his first roll and started on his second as she savored every bite of hers. She'd only ordered one, though she could easily have eaten more. She finished every last bite of an enormous side of coleslaw then sat back to sip at her soda and watch Gray finish his meal. They chit-chatted about inconsequential things while they relaxed and enjoyed the view of the harbor.

When the waitress stopped to check on them, Gray ordered two pieces of blueberry pie. "Did you want coffee?"

"*Oui.* Yes, please."

They sipped their drinks for a minute in a companionable silence before he spoke again. "My sister's trying to get clean again." He shrugged. "I don't know why, but something about this time feels different."

"That's wonderful." She squeezed his hand where it rested on the tabletop. Had her spell given him false hope, or had she actually helped his sister turn her life around? She desperately hoped the latter.

"She kicked the asshole to the curb and has a space at a rehab clinic reserved. I'm taking her there at the end of the month. I'd about given up. I hope I'm not being a blind idiot believing in her again."

"Believing in someone is always worthwhile. Sometimes that's all someone needs to have the courage to change themselves."

"Wise words."

"I have my moments." Her heart fluttered at the look in his eyes. She was falling hard for this man. At times like this, she thought he might return the feeling.

Their pie arrived and they fell silent once more. He scooped up a large bite of vanilla ice cream along with his pie and brought the fork to his mouth. "Oh, man. This really is fantastic. I usually like variety, but if I had to stick to one thing, this would be it."

One thing, huh? Were they still talking about the pie?

****

"Just ease your foot off the brake and…"

The car jerked forward. Isabeau slammed her foot on the brake and they shuddered to a stop. Gray put his hand over hers and moved the gear back into park. She heaved a sigh of relief.

"I'm terrible at this."

"Yes, you are."

He leaned against his headrest and laughed while she shot daggers at him with her glare. And they'd been getting along so well the past few weeks, too. When he'd suggested he take her for a driving lesson, she'd actually thought it was a good idea.

Fool.

"I don't like being confined in this tiny little box."

His laughter slowly died and he turned to her. He tucked a strand of hair behind her ear. He didn't remove his hand right away, instead left it to rest against the sensitive skin of her neck just below her ear. She hoped he assumed her pulse raced from her disastrous attempts to make his car go rather than his proximity.

Every instruction had come with a physical

demonstration with his hands. He was driving her insane.

"You work the gas and the brake with your right leg." He'd run his hand down her thigh to her knee and pressed gently until the engine roared like her heartbeat. "You adjust your rearview mirror like this." He'd cupped her hand around the mirror and leaned in so their heads were less than an inch apart.

Her nerves were so frazzled she kept forgetting what she was supposed to be doing. He'd ask if she had any questions, but the only one that came to mind was whether or not there was enough room for them to make love in the back seat. Probably not the response he expected.

"You can do this." He rubbed his thumb back and forth against her ear lobe. She practically purred and he finally noticed the affect his touch had on her. His gaze intensified until she couldn't look away. He was barely a hairsbreadth away, the heat of his minty fresh breath caressed her lips.

She strained forward that last tiny little bit. She kissed him. Or he kissed her. She didn't really care. She'd been thinking about what this would be like since he first walked into her shop.

He didn't disappoint. His lips were warm against hers. His touch gentle, yet demanding at the same time. As if they'd choreographed it, their mouths opened at the same instant and their tongues danced.

She'd longed for this moment. Her one hand was trapped between them, but she slid her other up his arm, caressing his taut biceps, then slipped forward to caress his chest. The starched material of his shirt crinkled in her hand, but did little to disguise the hard muscles beneath. She'd caught a glimpse or two of that bared chest in the time he'd stayed with her and had longed to feel herself pressed against him ever since.

His hand tightened in her hair. He deepened the kiss. Tendrils of desire curled through her, swirling in her stomach, tightening her chest and firing her insides. Wow.

The loud *chirp chirp* of a siren interrupted the haze of desire clouding her mind. She tore herself away and squinted at the light shining through her window. Sheriff Lawton-Mackenzie stood just outside her door with a flashlight. Isabeau dropped her head against the steering wheel, her face burned with embarrassment.

Gray chuckled and leaned across her to lower the window. "Hello, Sheriff. Is something wrong?"

The sheriff put a hand against her lips in a bid to hide her amusement. "Not at all. I was on my way home when I saw your car parked in the middle of the lot. Kids sometimes hang out here and like to get up to some mischief. You two causing any mischief tonight?"

"Trying to."

Isabeau gasped and aimed a punch at Gray's shoulder. She took a deep breath and faced the sheriff. "We're fine, thank you kindly. Gray is just giving me a driving lesson."

"Gray? As in Grayson Wright? I thought it was you."

Gray nodded, but didn't seem too pleased at being recognized.

"Lynn Lawton. I was a year behind you in school."

"Lawton? Ah, yes. Following in your father's footsteps I see." He didn't give her a chance to answer. "We were about done with our lesson anyway and should get back. Don't let us keep you."

He nudged Isabeau's shoulder, so she stepped out of the car and hurried around to the other side. After a few more words with the sheriff, he got in the driver's seat and took them back home.

Isabeau studied the passing scenery out her window. She couldn't face Gray after that kiss and the humiliation of being caught like an unruly teenager. What must he think of her? Had he kissed her or had she kissed him? The answer was of the utmost importance.

All she knew was she'd been unable to resist.

What was he thinking right now? She wished she could read his mind, but that kind of spell work was not to be used by decent people. The townsfolk would have been justified in burning her if she took part in that side of the craft.

She peeked at his profile from below lowered lashes. One arm lay casually across the door, the other draped over the steering wheel in a confident manner. He gazed straight ahead, eyes on the road. A smile played across his lips. He didn't appear to feel the tension that coursed through her body.

"The sheriff is lucky I don't carry a gun." He spoke quietly, but his words shocked her.

"What?"

His gaze darted toward her and away. His smile slipped but returned almost instantly. He wasn't as at ease as he appeared. She sucked in a breath at the heat from his gaze.

"Had I been armed, I likely would have shot her when she interrupted us." He flexed his hand around the steering wheel. "Still might, depending on what happens when we get back to your house."

****

Gray pulled into the driveway. What was Isabeau thinking? Did she regret that kiss? That perfect kiss?

Threatening to kill the sheriff for interrupting them hadn't been one of his smoother moves. Isabeau didn't appear amused by that little joke. Another response that didn't fall in line with the gold-digger theory. After all, if she were trying to seduce him, threatening murder over an interrupted kiss was a big hint that he was falling for her act.

He couldn't convince himself that was her goal anymore. She couldn't have faked that kiss, so full of innocence and lust. Lisa had been an accomplished actress, but every movement she made had been geared toward seduction and manipulation. Isabeau had simply kissed him back. There was no art to it, no calculation, just pure desire. The same as he'd felt. He couldn't be wrong about that.

Which meant she wasn't out to seduce him and was likely exactly what she appeared to be. A nice young woman who'd been kind to the old man who leased his house to her.

The thought should make him happy. But his body much preferred to think she was an accomplished seductress. Living in the same apartment with her *before* he knew what it was like to feel her pressed up against him had been tough enough. His body still wasn't completely under control. If she called an end to what began in the school parking lot, he'd have to find a new place to stay. Or spend the next few weeks taking cold showers twice a day.

He got out of the car and started to walk around to

open her door, but she leaped out and jogged toward the house before he had the chance.

Not a good sign.

Cold shower, here I come.

Eager to be close to her, but dreading it at the same time, he trailed behind. Hinting that he wanted to take things up where they'd left off in the car had been a bad idea. Now she was running scared. He should have been a gentleman and given her the option of pretending nothing had happened.

Screw that!

The screen door slammed shut behind him. No way was he pretending that kiss didn't happen. If she wanted to pursue it or not, that was her choice, but he couldn't let the chance slip by for the sake of possible embarrassment. If he'd let opportunities go just because they might not work out, he'd still be a stock boy rather than a self-made millionaire.

He found her at the kitchen sink, filling Havoc's water bowl.

She jumped. Water sloshed down her leg and onto the floor. Her hand trembled slightly as she set the bowl down. "I—I didn't hear you come in."

Enough small talk. They'd be here all day dancing around the issue. He yanked her into his arms and pressed a quick kiss upon her lips. Her eyes widened, but she didn't resist. A positive sign.

He kissed her again. Slower this time. Feeling her out. She responded immediately. Her hands slipped up his neck and gripped his hair. He wrapped his arms around her, let one hand drift down to grab her ass, lifting her up and into him.

They lost themselves in the pleasure of the

moment, secure in the knowledge no one would show up to interrupt them here. He wanted to shout in triumph. Instead, he steadied her against him and they made their way slowly down the hall toward her bedroom.

The door served as a barrier for less than a second. With a quick twist of the handle they were in the room. He lowered her to the bed, groaning when he lay full on top of her. She answered with a soft moan of her own that set his blood to roaring. Her restless hands roamed across his shoulders, along his sides, and then back to his hair.

His shirt stretched across his neck, choking him. It had to go. He propped himself up. The motion brought his length harder against her softness. His breath caught. He yanked his shirt over his head and threw it to the side. He let her examine him with tentative fingers that were sure to drive him insane. The clouded, lusty look in her eyes caused a growl to rise in his throat.

His fingers burned with the need to touch her soft skin. He wanted to feel her, everywhere. He cursed the tiny buttons of her flimsy blouse as he struggled to release them without tearing the delicate fabric. He wanted to rip it off her.

She put a hand to his chest. "Stop."

He let his eyes fall shut to hide his disappointment. Damn. So close.

He should be grateful she'd stopped him now. If he'd actually seen her naked, would he have been able to stop? He liked to think so, but the way frustration ate at his insides, he wasn't entirely sure.

She shifted so he eased back. He had to get the hell

off her.

"Gray?"

His eyes popped open at her hesitant tone. His jaw almost hit her stomach, she surprised him so much. She'd stripped off her shirt and bra. She stared up at him, her arm crossed over her breasts. Her other hand groped for the shirt she'd tossed to the side. Tears clouded her eyes. Her face burned beet red. "I thought…"

The hurt tone in her voice nearly undid him. He dipped forward for a quick kiss. He needed a second to collect himself. The relief that he'd mistaken her meaning was incredible. But he needed to repair the damage he'd done with his mistake.

He took both her hands in his and raised her arms above her head so he could look his fill. Damn. "You're beautiful," he whispered. He couldn't manage anything more.

The tension drained from her body. She softened beneath him. "You pulled away. I thought…"

"I thought you were telling me to stop. I thought I was going to die."

She giggled. "No. You were just taking too long with my shirt."

"Damn straight." He caressed her breast and caught her gasp in his mouth before saying, "You shouldn't be allowed to cover these."

"I might get some funny looks walking down the street topless."

"Only from lust or envy. Trust me."

"I do."

He refused to think about why those two words made his jaw clench.

Chapter Eight

The next morning, Isabeau threw on a Lobster Cove sweatshirt and jeans to take Havoc on his morning walk. A quick comb through her hair didn't cut it, so she shoved on a baseball cap to hide her bed head.

Thoughts of bed brought a huge smile to her lips. She'd only had two lovers prior to Gray, but he was certainly the most attentive and skilled. After their initial awkwardness, they'd come together remarkably well. She'd been somewhat disappointed to find him gone when she woke in the morning, but he was an early riser, so she tried not to read anything into it. He'd kept himself busy the entire time he'd stayed with her. Why would today be any different?

Still, she would have liked to spend the morning cuddled in bed learning more about her lover. Later. They'd have plenty of time.

Havoc yanked on his leash, bringing her attention back down to earth. "What is it?" The dog's hackles stood on end. His attention riveted on a doorway several feet in front of them. "Oh, no." She hadn't paid attention this morning. She usually turned down First Street to avoid this side of Ash Avenue. The door Havoc stared at belonged to Sherri Evard-Price.

And it was open.

Isabeau spun on her heel. She couldn't walk past

that door. Today was a good day. She didn't need to deal with Sherri spewing her vile accusations.

A startled yelp brought her to a stop.

"Help."

The weak cry came from the direction of Sherri's front stoop. Isabeau closed her eyes for the barest of seconds, gathered her courage, and headed toward the sound. She couldn't ignore it.

Sherri lay prostrate on the front stoop in the fetal position, hands clutching her stomach. Isabeau hoped the dark blotchy patches between her legs were from her water breaking and not something more ominous.

"Sherri!" Isabeau ran the last few steps. She dropped Havoc's leash, giving him a silent mental command to stay at her side. She whipped out her cell and dialed nine-one-one.

At the sound of Isabeau's voice, Sherri looked up with a groan. "Not you. Get away," she whispered, her hissed words barely discernible through her heavy panting.

Isabeau grabbed the hand Sherri feebly swatted at her. "Don't be stupid, Sherri. You need help."

When emergency services picked up, Isabeau told them Sherri's condition and address. She settled in at Sherri's shoulders, afraid to help the poor woman move, less she cause her more discomfort.

Between pants, Sherri said, "How do you live with yourself? Did you cast some spell on me, on him? Are you trying to kill me and the baby so you can steal my husband?"

Isabeau winced from Sherri's claw-like grasp on her arm, as well as her words. "I don't know what you mean, Sherri. I've never done anything to you. I would never try to hurt anyone. How many times do I have to tell you that I have no interest in Logan? Not to mention he's not interested in me." Why did Sherri have such a poor opinion of her husband?

Sherri's words turned incomprehensible, but the meaning was clear enough from her vicious tone of voice.

Isabeau had to do something. Logan had said the baby wasn't due until next month.

Isabeau let her anger over the accusations go. Sherri must be consumed with worry over her baby right now. The stress of having Isabeau be the one to help her wasn't doing her any good. But Isabeau couldn't just leave her here.

Havoc nudged the back of Isabeau's neck. A sense of calm flooded through her.

That's what Sherri needed. She needed to calm down. But that wasn't going to happen anytime soon. Who could blame the poor woman? Isabeau would call on her powers. She didn't have anything to aid the spell, so her voice would have to do. She wouldn't force a calming spell on Sherri anyway. Who knew what harm could be done inadvertently? And Sherri most definitely wasn't going to give Isabeau permission to cast a spell on her.

Instead, Isabeau would cast calming, healthy thoughts out on the wind. Hopefully, Sherri and the baby would pick up on them and welcome them into themselves.

> *"I ask for aid to do some good,*
> *to help this family if I could.*
> *A sense of calm is what I seek,*
> *to keep this pair from growing weak."*

Sherri's death grip on Isabeau's arm gradually loosened. Her tirade against all things Isabeau ceased. Isabeau gaped at Sherri's belly where the baby rolled from one side to the other. A sense of urgency hit her in the stomach. The baby wanted to be born now.

Isabeau sent her thoughts to the child. Tried to instill some patience. The baby's movements slowed and some of the urgency faded.

Lights flashed in her peripheral vision and she cried out in relief.

"I can see the ambulance. They're almost here." She wiped Sherri's hair out of her eyes.

"My baby. It's too early." Sherri sucked in a deep breath and stared hard into Isabeau's eyes. "Please. Don't do this. Don't hurt us. What did I ever do to you?" Tears ran like rivers down her cheeks. Her face paled as another contraction overcame her. She clenched her hands and moaned.

Sherri actually believed Isabeau wanted to kill her and the baby.

Isabeau sat in stunned silence as the EMT crew arrived and bustled about taking care of their patient. She managed the appropriate responses to their questions, but inside a part of her withered and died.

Sheila, the ambulance driver, paused to study Isabeau's face. "You okay? Why don't you ride with us?"

Sheila's gaze swiveled between Isabeau and the ambulance for a second as her partner secured Sherri in the rig. Isabeau could practically read the woman's thoughts. Sheila was good friends with Sherri—who had no doubt shared her mistaken belief that Isabeau wanted to seduce Logan away from his family. Sheila wouldn't want to put Sherri through the emotional trauma of sharing space with Isabeau.

But, Sheila also wouldn't want to leave Isabeau behind if she were hurt.

Isabeau shook her head. "I'm fine. Just a little unsettled. Take care of Sherri."

After one more uncertain look, Sheila nodded and raced to secure the ambulance doors. The siren's wailing slowly faded away.

Isabeau stared after the departing ambulance as she tried to comprehend what had just happened.

She'd always held out hope that a part of Sherri knew deep inside that Isabeau was a good person and incapable of such horrible deeds. Apparently not.

That Sherri was Heloise's reincarnation had been immediately obvious. But Isabeau's excitement had quickly turned to bafflement as Sherri took an immediate, and violent, dislike to Isabeau. There was no reason for it in the present day, so Sherri's feelings must be based on a residual memory from the past. Which meant that Heloise had believed that bastard fiancé of hers.

Why had Heloise helped Isabeau escape burning if she thought Isabeau had tried to seduce her fiancé with a spell?

Someone could have come up and kicked her in the gut at that moment and she'd barely notice. A ball of dread filled her. Why had she never put two and two together?

The spell hadn't gone wrong. In fact, everything had worked exactly as Heloise wished. Heloise knew how Isabeau longed to escape from Lobster Cove. So she'd made sure that would never happen.

Heloise hadn't saved her. She'd cursed her.

*****

Gray was eager to get home to Isabeau. He'd left her fast asleep before dawn this morning. She'd been so peaceful tucked up in bed and he wanted to spend the rest of the day in that bed with her.

But he'd promised to take Connie to the rehab clinic. He'd been gone longer than expected because Frank had shown up, pissed that Gray's lawyer had served him with divorce papers and insisting the whole thing was Gray's idea. He'd refused to listen to a word Connie said, even trying to drag her physically out of the clinic.

Luckily, the center had called the police the second Frank showed. The officers had witnessed his behavior and it looked like Frank was out of luck talking his way out of this one. With the director on Connie's side, Gray was finally confident Frank wouldn't be a factor in Connie's life much longer.

Ambulance lights flashed up ahead, followed quickly by the wail of its siren. Were they coming from Sherri's house?

What the hell?

Gray drove up as the ambulance pulled away, lights flashing, sirens blaring. They were moving pretty damn fast, somebody was in trouble. Shit, he hoped everything was all right with Sherri and the baby.

A loud *woof* brought his attention to the house. Havoc hovered over Isabeau, who slumped against Sherri's front door. Fear clogged his throat.

He jumped out of the car, leaving the motor running in case he needed to rush Isabeau to the emergency room. Why had the ambulance left without her?

Sweat soaked the front of her sweatshirt. Her hair trailed across her face, but she made no effort to push it out of her eyes. Trails of dried tears ran down her cheeks.

He crouched beside her, pulling her limp form into his arms. "Isabeau? Baby, what's wrong? Are you hurt?"

She didn't respond. He tapped her lightly on her pale cheek in an effort to snap her out of whatever had her in its thrall. He grabbed her ice-cold hand and brought it to his lips to blow some warmth onto it.

That's when he saw the blood.

"Jeez. You're bleeding." He propped her against his shoulder with one arm and reached for his cell. "I'm calling nine-one-one. Why the hell did the ambulance leave you like this?"

"Not my blood," she whispered. Her voice came out as a croak, as if she hadn't used it in days. Or as if she'd used it too much.

Had she called for help and no one came? He restrained himself from cursing the EMTs. He needed to help her now. He wouldn't be much use if he ran off half-cocked in a rage at those useless bastards.

He eased her into his arms and brought her to sit at the picnic table a few steps away.

"Whose blood is it?" Stupid question. He looked at his and Sherri's initials carved into the table and he knew. "Sherri? Is she okay? What happened?"

"The baby. She wanted to come early. But the doctors will be able to help. I think I convinced the baby to wait a little longer. At least until they reach the hospital."

He swept the hair out of Isabeau's face. "You're talking nonsense, honey. You must be in shock. I should get you to the hospital."

She shook her head. "Not nonsense. People think witches only do evil things. That's not true. 'And ye harm none.' That's what it's all about. Why don't people ever believe that?"

Her eyes pleaded with him to understand. He didn't. He struggled to find some way to pacify her until he could get help. "It's okay. I believe you." He winced at the lie, but it couldn't be helped. She'd understand when she was feeling better. He'd somehow explain the gnawing pain in his chest that refused to go away even though he knew the blood wasn't hers. Who wouldn't tell a few little white lies in the face of such a feeling?

He stood, propping her against his chest as she rose on unsteady legs. "Come on. It'll be faster if I drive."

Havoc whined deep in his throat and stood between him and the car.

"Out of the way."

The dog shifted on his haunches but didn't move.

Gray took a step forward, assuming Havoc would move to avoid being stepped on, and hopped to keep his balance while avoiding crushing the dog's toes. Havoc refused to move and gave a low growl. "Damn it, Havoc! I have to get Isabeau to the hospital. Out of the way." Now he was arguing with a dog. He was as out of his mind as Isabeau.

She wasn't helping either. Not only was she not making any attempt to keep up with him, but she fought to move away from the car. Her attempts were weak at best, but present nonetheless.

"Not going." Her head rocked back and forth so violently her hair whipped him in the eye and he had trouble keeping his arm around her.

"Yes, you are." He swung her up and caught her behind the knees so he could cradle her in his arms. If she was going to act like a baby about going to the hospital, he'd treat her like one.

Havoc's growl increased in volume and tone, very clearly telling him to shut up and sit down. One peek at the thick row of teeth and raised hackles and Gray took a step back to lower himself to the picnic bench, settling Isabeau gently in his lap.

Havoc immediately ceased his growling and sat. His tongue lolled out of his mouth, mocking triumph all over his face.

"Jeez, what the hell are you teaching that dog?"

He said it to himself, but Isabeau answered. "He knows I can't step foot in the hospital. He's protecting me."

When would she start making sense? "You're in shock. You need to see a doctor."

"Maybe. But the hospital is off limits."

"Why?"

"I always wondered why I couldn't go there."

"What are you talking about?"

"Because of Heloise. I never got the chance to explain what happened. I never thought she'd believe I was capable…"

Her sob tore at his heart. But he couldn't make any sense of her words. "Who's Heloise?"

"Sherri is Heloise. She doesn't remember, of course. Not many remember their past lives. But sometimes feelings come through. That's why she hates me."

He wished he could deny it, but he'd been shocked at how virulently Sherri disliked Isabeau. Hate didn't seem that far off. But a past life?

Isabeau's voice dropped to a whisper. He had to tilt his head in order to hear her.

"Heloise cursed me. And Sherri's subconscious remembers why. Heloise knew how much I hated L'Anse des Homards—Lobster Cove. I wanted to leave more than anything. When I saw her casting the circle, I thought she was helping me escape. That she knew I was innocent. But she wasn't. Our spells must have collided. Mine got me away from the fire, but hers trapped me in Lobster Cove."

Spells? She'd gone over the edge. He dialed nine-one-one.

"I need an ambulance. 88 Ash Avenue. A woman's gone into shock. She's speaking nonsense." He answered their questions, left the call open and set the phone on the table so he could return his attention to Isabeau. She hadn't stopped speaking the entire time he'd been on with the dispatcher.

"…wasn't my fault. I'd only gone to visit Heloise. I picked up the brush because it was so luxurious. I never had anything so fancy. I envied Heloise for all her beautiful things. But I wouldn't have taken it. I told *him* that when he found me in her room. He threatened me. Said he'd tell everyone he caught me stealing. Unless I kept quiet. But I couldn't let him…"

Ice encased Gray's chest followed swiftly by a blinding rage. He'd kill him. Whoever *he* was.

"I tried to push him off me. He was too strong." Her eyes were glazed over. She stared into the distance, but Gray doubted she saw anything other than her memory. "Sherri's mother walked in."

He started. "Sherri's mom?"

"No. No. I didn't mean Sherri. Heloise. It was Heloise's mother. And Rudolph accused me..." Her voice trailed off, her eyes were wide and unfocused, her lips pursed tight.

"Of what?"

"Witchcraft." She shuddered and fell silent.

****

Isabeau clamped her mouth shut. What had come over her? How much had she told him? He must think she'd gone completely insane.

"Witchcraft?"

She groaned. What should she say? She braced herself to look him in the eyes. Concern. Confusion. Disbelief. No hate—at least not yet. A part of her longed to confess the whole truth to him. Had she done it yet? She couldn't remember everything she'd said in her shock at realizing Heloise's betrayal.

Whatever she had said, he obviously didn't believe a word of it. He must think she'd gone through some kind of psychotic break.

"What—?" She had to clear her throat. "What did I say?"

He heaved a huge sigh. Of relief?

"A bunch of nonsense about spells and past lives. What happened? Is Sherri okay? Why did the EMTs leave you like this?" His voice hardened when he mentioned the medics. He snatched up his cell. The dispatcher's voice blared through the speaker giving a ten minute estimate. "Never mind, I'm bringing her in." He stuck the phone in his pocket.

"I don't need the hospital. And they had to take care of Sherri. There was no time to waste. I was fine. I just—"

"You were nowhere near fine. You were babbling nonsense. Your hands are covered in blood. You're white as a sheet. Why didn't they take you in the ambulance with Sherri?"

A bark of laughter erupted from her mouth. "There's no way Sherri would let me ride with her." She kept most of the bitterness out of her tone. It wasn't easy. Now that the initial shock had faded, anger boiled up. "She should have known better. We were best friends. I never would have done that to her."

"You and Sherri were friends?"

She couldn't fault his skeptical tone. No one who ever experienced the way Sherri reacted to Isabeau would think the two had ever been friends. She shook her head. "Not Sherri. Heloise."

His body tensed. She felt it all along her body since she sat in his lap. How had she gotten there? She would have been quite comfortable under other circumstances.

She stared at the blood staining her hands. Tried to wipe it off on her jeans, but the blood had dried and wouldn't come off. She choked back the bile at the back of her mouth. "I'm going to be sick."

Gray held her hair as she retched in the grass. Thankfully, she hadn't eaten breakfast before taking Havoc for his walk, so her stomach was empty.

When she finished, Gray helped her stand. He eased her into his car and she leaned against the headrest. "I could walk. My house isn't that far."

"I'm not taking you home." The car was already running. He threw it into gear and took off down the street.

Her eyes popped open. "Where are we going?"

Please, no.

"You can't take me to the hospital." Havoc's frantic barking quickly faded as they sped away. She spun in her seat to send her familiar a silent plea to go home, to stay safe.

"Why not? You're in shock. You need to see a doctor. Why are you so scared of hospitals?"

"Just this one. Heloise's house used to be there. I always wondered…" Heloise had wanted her stuck in Lobster Cove, but obviously she didn't want Isabeau anywhere near her. Why give her best friend a chance to explain? "She must have protected her house when she cursed me." The bitterness came out in her voice. Her heart hurt thinking about it. "I can go anywhere in town, but not into the space where her house used to be. I haven't been to that area since I was in nineteen twenty-nine. It was such a shock when I traveled. I'd thought I was safe within the town limits. I have no idea what year I ended up that time—it was before the land was settled." She wrapped her arms around her midsection. "I was all alone. Scared, cold, starving. I'd gotten used to heat and being able to eat whenever I wanted." She smiled. "Indoor plumbing. What a huge difference that makes." She should shut up. Let him put her outburst down to shock.

"You're scaring me, Isabeau." He clung to the steering wheel with a white-knuckled grip. His mouth pursed in a tight line as he stared straight ahead.

She squeezed his arm. "I apologize. It's certainly a lot to take in all at once. I can't seem to stop talking. I've kept this in for so long. Other than your uncle, I've had no one I could confide in."

Gray's arm jerked under her hand. "Uncle Stan?"

"Yes. Your uncle knew all about me. He was such an enormous help to me whenever I traveled within his lifespan."

The car jerked to a stop. They'd arrived at the emergency entrance to the hospital.

The trembling began in her hands, but soon enough she shook all over. Gray rounded the car and yanked open her door. She shrank back against the seat, but he overpowered her. He swung her into his arms and carried her through the sliding door.

He plunked her down in front of the nurse's station. "See. You're fine. I can't believe you thought I'd fall for such a crock of shit. My uncle was a good man. He didn't deserve to be taken advantage of like that."

His words brought her head up. "Stanley was my friend. I would never—"

"Was it your idea? Your mother's?"

"What are you talking about?"

"That picture. Your resemblance to your mother is incredible. How long did it take you to convince Uncle Stan that you were your mother? You must have concocted the scheme together. She'd have told you everything she knew about my uncle. What did you hope to gain? Did you think he'd marry you? Or forsake me and leave you all his money?"

Whack! Her palm stung from the slap. Through a haze of fury, she had the satisfaction of seeing the red print of her hand on his cheek, but she'd swung her hardest and barely moved him. "I loved Stanley. He was my friend. How dare you." Her voice shook with the force of her emotion.

She swung around, but an old woman in a wheelchair blocked the entrance. Isabeau swiveled in the other direction and took off down the hall. She had to get away. First Heloise's betrayal and now Gray. She couldn't take anymore.

"Isabeau," he called after her.

She kept going.

An electric jolt screamed through her limbs. The white tile with the blue stripes along the edges disappeared, replaced with hard packed dirt and occasional patches of weeds. The smell of horse manure replaced the antiseptic cleanliness of the hospital.

She staggered to a stop. Her head swiveled, trying to figure out when she'd ended up. The view was eerily familiar. Had she been to this point in Lobster Cove history before?

Her gaze on the buildings lining the dirt road, she took a step back and twisted her ankle. She turned to see what had tripped her up and fell to the ground. Shock froze her limbs. Roaring like a waterfall filled her ears.

She'd tripped on a lone piece of charred wood that had somehow fallen from the huge pile before her.

Yeah, she'd been to this time before. And they hadn't even had time to clean up the pyre where they'd tried to burn her.

Chapter Nine

Gray blinked.

What the hell?

Isabeau had disappeared right before his eyes. One minute she'd been storming away from him. The next, she was gone. Not a trace.

He ran down the long corridor searching for a door. Had she slipped through an exit? But there were no doors off the hall. Even if there had been, he knew what he'd seen. She hadn't walked out of the way. She'd vanished.

Holy crap.

She'd warned him. Or tried to. Of course he hadn't believed her insane story about time travel. No one would have believed her.

He thought of Uncle Stan's crazy talk right before his death. Not so crazy after all.

He stumbled back down the hallway. His legs shook. He needed to sit before he fell flat on his face. Not only had he called her a liar, he'd accused her of trying to con his uncle.

She was innocent. And he loved her. Now he'd lost her.

He was an idiot.

He grabbed a corner of the nurse's station to prop himself up, ignoring the RN's concerned gaze. A hand grabbed his shoulder. He spun around. Logan stared at him in confusion.

"You okay, Grayson? Are you here to see Sherri?" Logan narrowed his eyes as he scrutinized Gray's face.

Gray couldn't imagine what he saw. Was "idiot" written across his forehead? Why else would Logan, whom he barely knew, take such an interest in a virtual stranger when his wife was in labor?

"I'm fine."

Liar.

Logan didn't buy it either. He grabbed Gray's arm and guided him to the waiting room. The screech of the cheap plastic chair assaulted Gray's ears as Logan forced him to sit. "You're obviously not fine. You're white as a ghost. Are you hurt?"

Gray swatted at Logan's hands checking for his pulse. "I said I'm fine." He leaned forward to rest his head in his hands. His temples pounded like fists upon a closed door. "Oh, God. Isabeau," he whispered. "Where did you go?" Where? The question should be when. His stomach knotted, the perfect accompaniment to his monster headache.

"What happened to Isabeau?"

Logan's concerned voice broke into Gray's melancholy thoughts. What should he tell him? What would people think when Isabeau was nowhere to be found?

"It's nothing. She was pretty upset when she found Sherri. I brought her here, but she ran off."

"Should we go talk to her? I can let her know Sherri and the baby will be fine."

"What? Oh, the baby. That's good. Good."

"You're obviously upset, too. Stay here and get a hold of yourself. I'll go find Isabeau."

Of all the...

"You are unbelievable. Do you really think Isabeau needs to see *you* at a time like this? She's the one who called the ambulance to rush your wife to the hospital. That can't have been easy for her. And now, rather than taking care of your wife, you want to run off to comfort your girlfriend."

"My what?"

Gray's head jerked back. Logan's fury hit him like a jab to the face.

Fists clenched at his sides, face red and eyes bulging—Logan was a lit fuse ready to blow. He grabbed the front of Gray's shirt and hauled him up so they stood toe to toe.

"I'm a married man. Isabeau and I are friends. Nothing more. I'd appreciate it if you kept your despicable lies to yourself."

Gray's heart stopped. He'd been wrong about that too. How many other mistakes had he made with Isabeau? He needed to run after her to apologize. But he couldn't. He'd already chased her away. And where she'd gone, he couldn't follow.

There was only one thing he could do. Get her back. He'd find a way.

Logan still held him in a death grip. Gray was lucky the man hadn't decked him. He deserved it.

He held out a hand. "I'm sorry, man. I've been a little crazy where Isabeau's involved. I don't know what the hell's wrong with me. I should have known the truth."

"You don't deserve her if that's what you think of her."

Gray couldn't argue with that. "You're right." He

let his hand drop back to his side.

Logan dropped Gray with a groan and ran his hand through his thinning hair. "Has Sherri heard these rumors? Is that why she acts so nuts whenever Isabeau's name is mentioned?"

"Yeah. Sorry, man." He hesitated. Dare he mention the cause? If everything else Isabeau had said was true—and he could no longer deny it after seeing her disappear with his own eyes—then her thought about Sherri's past life was probably real also. But how to suggest it without coming across as a complete whack job? "I hate to say it, but…"

Logan appeared expectant. "But…?"

"You're gonna think I'm nuts." He sighed.

Here goes nothing.

"Isabeau says they knew each other in a past life and Sherri's subconscious, or whatever, remembers and hates Isabeau." He forced himself not to cringe as he waited for Logan's answer. Gray wasn't disappointed.

Logan's jaw dropped. His eyes widened. He cast a nervous glance over his shoulder. "That's—"

"I know. It sounds crazy. I was right there with you when Isabeau told me. But now? I'm not so sure. I mean, I've seen some things…" He shook his head. He shouldn't go into what he'd seen. If for no other reason than Isabeau had confided in *him*, not Logan. The only other person she'd ever told… He snapped his fingers. "Uncle Stan!"

Logan jerked. He clearly thought Gray was out of his mind. There was no mistaking the expression on his face. Gray had probably looked about the same when Isabeau opened up to him.

He didn't have time to worry about that now. "I've

gotta go." He avoided Logan's half-hearted attempt to block his path and raced out to his car.

His parking job left much to be desired. He'd cut off half the entrance door in his attempt to get Isabeau seen to as quickly as possible. He'd been so furious thinking she'd used him, he'd barely been able to see straight.

He rounded the car's hood and jerked to a stop. Havoc stood beside the driver side door. His jowls quivered and his deep-throated growl caused the hairs on Gray's arms to stand on end. He held his hands palm up to the dog. "I didn't know. I thought she needed medical attention. I was trying to help her."

Great, now I'm pleading with a dog.

Maybe it wasn't such a bad strategy after all. Havoc cocked his ears as if considering Gray's words, then plopped his rear on the pavement and ceased growling. Gray approached cautiously, telling the dog what he planned to do next. He felt like a moron, but he couldn't deny the dog appeared to listen to every word.

Gray opened the door, frowning when Havoc jumped across the driver side and settled into the passenger's seat. The huge dog looked ridiculous, his rump on the seat, front paws on the floorboard. He twisted to stare at Gray, as if to say, "Hurry up."

Gray slid into his seat. The bank was just down First Street from the hospital, so the drive didn't take long. All the paperwork was in the glove box of the car, so he grabbed what he needed, then went in. Havoc followed behind and plopped down right outside the glass doors. A woman using the ATM on the right yelped when Havoc brushed against her leg.

"Sorry. He's friendly. I'll be right back." Gray

ignored her spluttering and entered the bank.

His hands trembled atop the safe deposit box lid while he waited for the assistant manager to give him some privacy. All his hope lay within the wide metal box on the table before him. What if his uncle hadn't been as curious as Gray remembered? What if he'd simply accepted Isabeau's time travel tales and let it be?

No. He wouldn't. Uncle Stan had never been one to let a matter rest. He'd always wanted to know how things worked. He wouldn't have been able to ignore a curse, magick, and time travel. He'd have investigated the shit out of the problem until he knew everything possible.

The door closed behind him. He eased the lid open and lowered it gently to the table. A large manila envelope lay inside. Stuffed to the gills, the flap strained against the metal clasp.

He struggled to get the package out of its container without ripping. He wanted to tear it open, but a feeling of dread stopped his hand. A cold draft from a ceiling vent sent a shiver down his neck. This wasn't right.

He hugged the package tight to his chest and left the bank. He and Havoc jumped in his car and headed down Pine Avenue toward home.

****

"Oh, God. No." Isabeau stumbled back from the pyre. This couldn't be happening. All the times she'd jumped back and forth through time, she hadn't come back once. She'd never thought to see these sites again. Wasn't that the point of her spell? To get away? Even though things hadn't worked out exactly as she'd planned, she thought she'd at least gotten that part right.

Apparently not.

The sun sat just above the horizon. If she weren't so appalled, she might stop to admire the sunset. Now she was just thankful that folks around here got to bed early. As long as she avoided the tavern, strangely enough in the same area that Murphy's bar was at home, she should be able to avoid detection.

First, she needed to get her bearings. It had been a long time since she'd been here and Lobster Cove was a completely different place in this time period.

Fewer trees for one. The L'Anse des Homards settlers hadn't been concerned about preserving nature. They'd clear cut most of the area, using the trees for their homes and businesses. None of the pretty shade trees she'd gotten used to in the modern version of town. Rather than a lovely park with trees and perfectly manicured lawn, the center of town here was a gathering spot with nothing to obstruct the view. The perfect spot for a witch burning. She shuddered at the memories that assaulted her as she swept her gaze over the pyre and out toward the bay.

Ned's Lobster Shack would be just over there. She'd eaten there so many times, she spotted its location with ease. So she stood right about where the gazebo would be. Murphy's Bar would be behind and to her left. She should have known. The curse always brought her back to the spot where she'd narrowly avoided a fiery end.

She turned to see and sure enough, the highest concentration of light in the area came from the lanterns outside the saloon. One of the many hypocrisies in the pious lifestyle of her home time. No matter what the men preached to any and all, the tavern always had a rousing business.

Well, rousing for such a small town. Murphy's Bar definitely had a larger crowd on a Wednesday than what she could see going on at the tavern tonight.

Still, best to get as far away from any sort of crowd as possible. She'd already been standing still for far too long. She couldn't afford to be seen. In her jeans and sneakers, she'd stick out like a sore thumb. She'd be recognized in an instant. And nothing would make the townsfolk happier than finding out the witch had returned.

She jogged toward the outskirts of town, trying to move as quick as possible without making any noise. She needed time to think out her next move—without the threat of discovery looming over her head.

Her ears strained to pick up any sound other than her own labored breathing and swift steps.

Was that a sneeze? She came to a dead stop, staring off into a row of bushes to her right. The mayor's house. Another fine, upstanding Lobster Cove gentleman. He hadn't so much as asked her a question before condemning her as a witch.

Of course, he'd been good friends with Heloise's fiancé. Even if he hadn't been, he never would have believed someone of Isabeau's social status over a wealthy member of their small society. The man craved power like any modern day politician, and that didn't come from a washerwoman's daughter.

Silence met her ears. Nothing moved beyond the hedge. She must have imagined it.

She continued on her way, the safety of the woods a mere ten feet away. She was going to make it.

"Isabeau Munier!"

Her name spit out with such hatred from the voice of her dearest friend nearly brought her to her knees.

Heloise.

Isabeau swiveled on her heels, bracing herself to face Heloise's ire. Still, the rage Isabeau saw in her former friend's expression tore at her heart.

"Heloise," she whispered. Tears choked her voice. She wanted to rush into her friend's loving embrace, but Heloise's livid expression made it clear Isabeau wasn't welcome. How had it come to this?

Isabeau took a step forward, but stopped herself. Heloise had practically shouted her name. Any minute now, someone might overhear them and she'd never get the chance to explain. Her heart cringed that she even needed to. How could Heloise believe the lies her fiancé told? She barely knew the man, yet she and Isabeau had been friends since they were three.

So Isabeau edged toward the shelter of trees so close behind her. She'd take it as a good sign Heloise seemed determined to follow. That she hadn't yelled for someone to drag Isabeau back to the woodpile, even better. Maybe a part of Heloise suspected the truth and wanted to give Isabeau a chance.

"How could you?" Heloise yelled in French, the words taking a moment to become clear to Isabeau—Lobster Cove hadn't been a French-speaking town for hundreds of years. "You were my friend. Why would you do such a thing? You knew how pleased I was with the match my father made for me."

Isabeau put a finger to her lips, shook her head, and gestured for Heloise to follow. She didn't give her a chance to refuse, just spun around and made for the trees.

She didn't need to look back to know Heloise followed. Heloise made no effort to hide her steps or quiet her voice. She stalked Isabeau, all the while blasting her for being a harlot and a traitor.

Isabeau winced. Her blood rushed through her veins and anger clouded her vision. She'd done nothing wrong. She didn't deserve this. Heloise should have trusted her. Should have known Isabeau would never do any of the awful deeds the townspeople had laid at her feet.

Because the second Isabeau had been accused of witchcraft, the people of L'Anse des Homards had blamed every misfortune any of them had ever experienced at her door.

The ten feet of snow the previous winter that had caused the church roof to collapse? Isabeau's fault. God wouldn't suffer a witch to shelter beneath his roof.

The storm that destroyed five homes along Lobster Cove's shores? Isabeau once again. The Talbert boy claimed Isabeau had tried to seduce him and brought destruction upon his home and the others in retribution when he refused her advances. In reality, the boy had been a thorn in Isabeau's side for years. Ever since Isabeau's body gained a few curves.

Heloise knew that. Why didn't she recognize the lies for what they were?

Finally. Isabeau stepped into the shelter of the trees. She took a moment to let her eyes adjust to the deeper blackness of the woods. Without the moon and stars to light her way, she could barely make anything out. At least she wouldn't have to see the look of condemnation on Heloise's face.

But she could still hear. "Heloise. Shut up." She

could only imagine Heloise's shock. Isabeau had never in her life raised her voice to her friend. Heloise had been the leader in their little duo.

"How could you believe I would ever do that to you? I assumed you were trying to help me. All these years, that was my one consolation. But, you cursed me? How could you?"

"Years? A week. A week in which I have had to face the humiliation of knowing my best friend betrayed me. That my betrothed was easy prey to a witch's spell."

It was too much. Isabeau stepped so close the scent of Heloise's unwashed body made her fight against gagging. She'd gotten used to twenty-first century hygiene.

She poked Heloise's skin-and-bones chest. "Your betrothed tried to rape me. He'd lay with a sheep if it baa'd at him and shift the blame to someone else. He's a horrible person and you'd be better off without him. But, unfortunately for me, I had no idea at the time. I didn't think twice about being alone with him, because he was your man. Until he reached for my skirts and laughed when I threatened to scream." Tears burned a path down her cheeks.

"I—I…" Heloise took several steps back until she stood on the edge of the wood. A shaft of light from the full moon illuminated her face.

Through her fury, Isabeau noticed a spark of pain in Heloise's eyes. "Why did you believe him?" she whispered.

Heloise crumpled. Her face screwed up until her eyes were mere slits. Tears poured down her cheeks. Her chest heaved with sobs.

Isabeau grabbed her before she fell to the ground, stumbling under the young girl's weight. She did her best to ease Heloise to the ground and leaned her against a tree.

Heloise doubled over, her face hidden behind her hands. Isabeau strained to hear her former friend's muffled words.

"I don't know. You're right. I should never have believed Rudolph. I—I just didn't want to believe the man I was to marry could be so horrible. He told me he caught you trying to steal my hairbrush. I'd seen you admire that brush. You wanted all that I had. I knew how much you envied my possessions. Rudolph claimed you tried to seduce him to keep your secret, and when he resisted your efforts, you cast a spell. He pretended to love me. I see now that was all a lie. My life is ruined. What am I to do?"

Isabeau gritted her teeth. Had Heloise always been so abominably self-centered? So childish? *Her* life was ruined? She'd cursed her best friend because she refused to see the truth. The truth had been too inconvenient. Isabeau had always thought of Heloise as mature and poised. How wrong she'd been.

Fifteen years of living on her own, traveling through time, had certainly aged Isabeau. Given her a completely different perspective on life. She was no longer the lonely, poor, teenager who envied her best friend.

She also didn't have time for this crap. "Heloise. Stop. Calm down."

Heloise continued to sob like her life was ending.

So Isabeau slapped her. Hard.

It felt good. After everything Heloise had put

Isabeau through, this very little bit of payback was just a drop in the bucket, but it would have to be enough.

The tears stopped abruptly. Heloise raised her red-rimmed eyes to stare at Isabeau in shock. Thinking about how Heloise's family doted on their only daughter, Isabeau was quite sure no one had ever raised a hand to her in her life. She'd led a charmed life until recently.

Isabeau's anger faded away. She sighed. "I'm sorry, but you needed to calm down. You'll be fine. Kick Rudolph to the curb and all your problems are solved."

"I don't understand your meaning." Heloise hiccupped mid-sentence, but at least she'd stopped crying.

Apparently Isabeau had picked up some twenty-first century vocabulary. Adjusting to a new time always took her a while. She repeated herself in words Heloise would understand. "Break off your betrothal to Rudolph. Use me as an excuse. Say you cannot marry someone who is so susceptible to witchcraft. Then marry someone else. You always had plenty of beaus. Like that Evard boy." Isabeau knew from her research that this is exactly what happened. She'd assumed because Heloise was on her side and wouldn't marry the monster that accused her best friend of witchcraft. Apparently not. "I never understood why your family chose Rudolph in the first place."

"I wanted him, so Father arranged the match." Heloise stood on shaky legs. She brushed at her skirts, setting them to rights. Whether or not she succeeded was unclear in the dark.

"*You* picked him?" Isabeau thought back to those

days. She supposed it made sense. Rudolph was young and reasonably attractive. He had a nice home, pleasant family. On the surface he must have seemed like a good catch when the other options in their town were a bunch of dour-faced, middle-aged men. And Heloise wouldn't have dug much deeper than appearance and family. "Well, then your father will likely have no problem dissolving the betrothal."

"I can't speak of such things to my father," she exclaimed, the horror clear in her tone.

Isabeau rolled her eyes. "Then enjoy being Madame Rudolph Friant. Now, if you'll excuse me, I have to run away before the townsfolk get their wish and burn me at the stake." She swung around and stalked through the trees. The swinging slap of a branch stung her cheek. She cursed and slowed her pace. The night was too dark to flounce away in a huff.

****

Havoc plopped onto the sofa the second Gray let him in Isabeau's house. The air felt chilled with her absence. She'd only been gone a short time, yet already the home felt abandoned. The air was stale, her fragrance gone.

Gray settled next to the dog and placed the envelope on the coffee table before them. His hand trembled as it hovered above the clasp.

So much rode on the contents of this package. What if it didn't contain what he hoped? How would he get Isabeau back with nothing to go on? He had no idea where she'd gone. And no idea how to begin the search.

He clenched his fist, took a deep breath, and then tore open the clasp. He shook the contents out onto the table.

A thick, leather-bound book took up the majority of the space. He picked it up and leafed quickly through the pages. Uncle Stan's handwriting covered every inch of the paper.

A smaller envelope contained pictures, loose papers covered in what appeared to be genealogy charts, and more pages full of Uncle Stan's writing.

This would take forever. He itched to do something other than read through his uncle's notes. Something active. Something decisive. Preferably something that would bring Isabeau into his arms in the next five minutes.

Havoc gave a soft *woof.* Gray scratched between the dog's ears as he contemplated the piles of information before him. This mess wasn't going to work itself out. He grabbed the notebook and read Uncle Stan's notes.

He wrote of watching Isabeau disappear from his car shortly after they met for the first time. Then detailed each time she reentered his life, sometimes years apart, yet each time she hadn't aged nearly as much as he had. That's when he called upon a friend at the historical society to dig up everything she could find on Isabeau Munier.

That friend was his Aunt Aggie. The love of Uncle Stan's life. She'd helped him find out all they could about Isabeau's travels. Then she'd found a way to keep Isabeau rooted in one time.

Several pages were ripped out of the book, the next one blank. Gray stared at the jagged edges of the paper. No. Not possible. Why the hell...?

His heart nearly stopped. The pain in his chest that had started the moment he saw Isabeau disappear grew to unbearable proportions. His breath came in short gasps.

Havoc whined. He swung his head over and dropped it with a thud in Gray's lap.

The heavy weight brought him back to his senses. That, and the wet heat of Havoc's tongue on the back of his hand.

"Damn, Havoc." He wiped his hand on his pants, then got back to business. There had to be something in his uncle's notes. Why would he have left these papers for Isabeau if they were useless?

He braced himself and flipped through the loose pieces of paper.

It has to be in here. Has to.

He quickly scanned through to the last page.

No. Impossible.

"I must have missed it, Havoc. There has to be something here." He tapped the jumbled papers back together into a neat pile. "I went through it too fast. There's a solution here. There has to be." He inhaled through his nose, breathed out through his mouth. He repeated the process ten times before focusing on the book once more.

He painstaking picked through the loose papers. An in-depth guide to Lobster Cove's history. He doubted Mr. Custer from Lobster Cove High knew half the stuff that had happened in this town. At least, he hadn't taught any of it when Gray had been in school. Crazy to think that Isabeau had experienced everything detailed in his uncle's notes. He couldn't picture her as a maid for the Rockefellers in the 1890's or as a hippie shouting make love not war in the sixties.

Yet, Uncle Stan had written down her accounts of

all of it. Gray couldn't *not* believe it. Not anymore.

Only a few more pages to go. He rubbed his eyes. The print wavered in front of him. He'd been at it for hours. Full dark had fallen, thankfully relieving him from the glare of the sun's rays through the window, but making him long for bed. Forget it. He'd never be able to sleep. Not without finding a way to get Isabeau home first.

Havoc nudged his arm. His big eyes reproaching him for resting even for a moment. "I know, Boy. I miss her already. But we'll get her back."

Not if his uncle's notes didn't come through.

He flipped a page and stared at the closely printed lines of script. The words flowed together, he couldn't make sense of them. Several lines were crossed out with notes written above in tiny, almost illegible, print.

A grouping of letters finally formed into something he could comprehend. Sherri's name, followed closely by Heloise. Isabeau had mentioned a connection between the two. He hunched closer to the page. On first glance, it appeared to be a recounting of Isabeau's arrival in this time. He was about to skim through the rest when he realized what he thought was just a blot on the page was actually a star, followed by a note in his aunt's handwriting.

A surge of excitement swept away the cobwebs that had been messing with his mind.

He might have found the answer.

****

"Isabeau, stop," Heloise called after her. "Please."

Slowly, Isabeau turned back to her old friend. "What?"

"I am sorry. My curse was childish, I know. Please

forgive me."

Isabeau ran a hand through her hair, tried to gather it into some semblance of order. She'd lost her cap somewhere along the line and her hair was out of control. She searched her pockets for a ponytail holder but came up empty and gave up. She avoided Heloise's gaze, unsure how to respond. Did she forgive her?

Heloise twisted her hands together in a motion Isabeau remembered well. A sure sign of her anxiety. In general, Heloise stayed as still as the perfect society darling her mother had trained her to be. Only when she felt something really deeply did she betray herself with such excess movement.

Isabeau sighed. "I do. I forgive you." Her heart lightened with the peace from a burden she hadn't wanted to face. Heloise's betrayal had been like a festering wound that had only now come clean.

Heloise took a tentative step forward. Isabeau wanted to run and grab her best friend in a warm embrace. She wanted to forget all that had happened. But she couldn't. Nothing would ever be the same. Starting with letting Heloise come to her rather than the other way around.

Moonlight filtered through the trees, enough so she could see the surprise in her friend's gaze. Throughout their friendship, Heloise had always led the way in everything. Isabeau followed around in her wake.

No more.

Their hug was brief. Too much had passed between them to return to their former comfort with one another. Relief rushed through Isabeau when Heloise allowed the hug to drop after only a few seconds.

Heloise's eyes widened and she stifled a gasp when

they separated. "You look so different." Her gaze swept over Isabeau from head to foot, causing her eyes to widen further.

Isabeau covered her mouth to hide her silent laughter. She imagined she'd done much the same when she stumbled into the twentieth century and caught sight of hippies in their fringe vests and bell-bottom jeans. Her pants were anything but immodest for modern times, but downright scandalous when most in this community tried to pretend women didn't have actual legs unless they were married—and even then, only the husband knew about them.

"I *am* fifteen years older."

"And yet only a week has passed for me." As if suddenly realizing the dangers of being seen with a known witch, Heloise cast her gaze back toward the village. "Your disappearance has the town in an uproar. I only barely managed to escape persecution myself. Some thought I contributed to your escape."

Isabeau frowned. "About that. Why did you? Why bother cursing me at all? You could have simply not cast the circle. I doubt I would have been able to make the spell work in unprotected space. I would have burned."

"I did not wish for you to die for your sin. Nor our village to suffer for completing such a heinous act." Heloise seemed genuinely surprised that Isabeau needed to ask the question.

Perhaps Heloise had reason. What would Isabeau have done were the situations reversed? She had to remember that, while Isabeau had aged fifteen years in the time she'd been gone, Heloise was but a week older. She was still a sixteen-year-old girl who had never been denied anything in her young life. That she cared what happened to this town spoke volumes for her sweet nature. And that she was still just a teenager.

"Of course." How silly of her.

"But now I fear for what they may do were they to see you once more. You must run from here. But you mustn't stay in any of the neighboring villages. Men were sent to warn of your escape."

"It doesn't matter. Once I cross the county line, I'll simply travel to another time." She sighed. Just when she'd found a time she would have happily lived the rest of her life. No other time would have the same appeal. No other time would have Gray. She brushed aside a tear that leaked down her cheek.

Perhaps that was for the best. Better to be in another time than watch Gray continue his life without her and face his disdain each time she saw him. Were she to make her way back to him, would he even have her? Should she attempt to trigger the curse until it brought her back to him?

"But the curse has ended," Heloise said.

Isabeau gaped at her. "What?"

"The curse ended the moment you returned to this time."

Isabeau's legs gave out. There was no going back.

Chapter Ten

Gray hesitated outside Sherri's hospital room door, his uncle's book clutched in one hand, tight to his chest. A bag of supplies from Isabeau's house hung from his wrist. He'd just seen the nurse, followed by Logan, wheel the baby out of the room. Sherri'd be alone. Now was the time. What if she refused to help?

He wasn't getting anywhere standing in the hall. He took a deep breath before inching the door open. "Sherri?"

"Gray. Come in," she said. Her smile was welcoming, but the bags under her eyes showed just how exhausting the last few hours had been. "You just missed Logan and the baby."

"Everything went well then? You and the baby are okay?"

"We're fine. Baby Heloise will have to stay in the hospital a few days, but she'll be fine."

His heart skipped a beat. "Heloise?"

She nodded. "It's an old family name."

"Yeah, I know."

Her eyebrows rose straight to her hairline.

"I'll explain later." He waved off any questions. "First, I need your help." He placed the book on her tray table with the bag of supplies next to it. "Isabeau's in trouble."

He waited for the sneer, or a snide comment,

prepared to defend Isabeau against Sherri's unreasonable hatred, but her face merely crinkled with confusion. "How can I help?"

A reasonable question. He hadn't expected her to be reasonable. "That's it? No—why should I care? Serves the bitch right? Nothing?"

She blushed. "I suppose I deserve that. I don't know why she drove me so crazy. I've never been the jealous type—I've always trusted Logan. I finally talked to him about her, and he explained everything. I never should have doubted him." She twirled a diamond bracelet on her arm. "She helped Logan earn enough money selling some old trinkets so he could buy me this beautiful bracelet. I've wanted it for the longest time."

He gave the jewelry a cursory glance. What did he care? But a pang of guilt hit him square in the chest. That's what Isabeau had been doing the day he jumped to the conclusion she was having an affair with a married man.

He'd just jumped from one stupid conclusion to another with her hadn't he? If he did manage to get her back, would she want anything to do with him?

He had to try, no matter how things worked out between the two of them. It was his fault she was gone. If it weren't for him, she never would have gone to the hospital in the first place.

Fear tightened his gut. Where had she gone? What was she suffering right now? Uncle Stan's notes had detailed much of Isabeau's travels. She hadn't always ended up in the most pleasant of times. She'd had to stumble around in the middle of a Mount Desert Island snowstorm for days one time when she'd arrived before the land had been settled.

He had to get her home. The sooner the better.

"I'm glad you've buried that hatchet because I think you're the only one who can help me."

"You still haven't told me what's wrong."

"Yeah. I'm getting to that. You're gonna think I'm crazy, but this is the truth." He placed Uncle Stan's notes in her hand and encouraged her to flip through them while he explained everything that he'd learned.

She took it better than he could have hoped. "You're right. You're crazy," she said when he finally stopped talking.

"I know. I'm in love." There. He'd finally admitted it. To the wrong woman, but still—This was a big moment for him. He'd never felt anything like this before. He'd tried to deny it, but couldn't anymore. Now he wanted more than anything for Isabeau to know how he felt.

"Uncle Stan's notes say the spell needs to be cast by someone with magickal blood. You're descended from the woman who cursed Isabeau in the first place. I don't know anyone else who could fit that description." She didn't look convinced, so he continued his plea. "I'll do everything else. I just need you to say the words. Please."

After an agonizing sixty seconds, she nodded. "Fine."

Relief swept through him, followed swiftly by anxiety. What if this didn't work?

****

Isabeau covered her face with her hands to hide her face from Heloise. She couldn't stifle her sobs, or still her shaking shoulders. Heloise knelt at her side, patting her back in that awkward way of someone who has no idea what to do.

"We shall find a way to see you safely away from here. Everything will be all right," Heloise whispered. She repeated the mantra several times.

Isabeau tried to ignore her, but she wouldn't give up. Finally, Isabeau couldn't stand it anymore. "No. It won't. I can't get back. He'll go on with his life, and I'll spend the rest of my life scraping to get by with only memories of the man I love. How is that all right?" She swiped angrily at her tears. This was useless. Railing away at Heloise didn't help either. The girl was still a child. What did she know about love? Or loss?

Heloise sank down on the ground beside Isabeau with a thoughtful expression on her face. "You fell in love in the future? Does your man feel the same about you?"

"No. Yes. Maybe. I was beginning to hope he might care for me, but everything fell apart right before I stepped back to this time." She wiped her nose surreptitiously on her sleeve. Heloise was likely appalled by such unladylike behavior, but Isabeau was beyond caring.

"Do you believe he will strive for your safe return? Will he search for you?"

Isabeau shook her head. "I don't know. Why? What are you getting at?"

"Were his heart searching for yours, there may be the possibility of crafting a spell to bring you together once more."

A faint stirring of excitement in her chest straightened Isabeau's spine.

Could there be a way?

She shouldn't get her hopes up, but... "What would we need to do?"

"First we must gather up supplies. When the time is right, we shall reach out to your man and pray to the God and Goddess he receives our call."

****

Gray scrutinized the candles placed in a circle around Sherri. He shot a glance at the door, checking that the nurses were still gathered around their station gossiping about the new doctor in town. They looked like they were just warming up to the subject, so he probably had some time. Still, once he lit the candles they'd have to hurry with the spell.

He wanted to get this over with for Sherri's sake, too. Dark circles shadowed her eyes, her hair resembled a bird's nest, and her chin kept dropping toward her chest. He'd encouraged her to sleep while he got things set up, but he wasn't sure she'd managed any more than ten minutes.

Should he wait? Was he being an asshole putting her through this so soon after a very difficult birth? All he needed her to do was read a few lines of poetry, what harm could that do?

Her chin touched her chest and she jerked upright. She stared around the room with eyes round as an owl's.

"Maybe we shouldn't do this," he said.

She rubbed her eyes and yawned. "I'm fine. I want to help."

"We can wait until tomorrow." He rubbed the back of his neck. He didn't want to wait. Everything in him screamed to get Isabeau back now. He could imagine only too well all the things that could go wrong in the past. Yeah, she was used to time traveling, she'd done it so many times—she'd survive. But all the notes in Uncle Stan's books showed she'd gone through hell. The thought was killing him.

"No. You said Isabeau's in danger. I'd feel horrible if something happened to her because I wanted to take a nap." She shook her head. "No. We're not waiting. Light the candles."

Chapter Eleven

Isabeau pressed her back against the rough-hewn logs of Mr. Fistwell's house. Her heart raced as she waited for the signal to make her move. She only had to cross the dirt-packed road to Heloise's back door, but the clouds had virtually disappeared and the moon had come out of hiding. For folks not used to electric lights, it was practically bright as day. If anyone happened to peer out their window, she'd be caught.

She couldn't afford that. They wouldn't wait 'til morning to light the pyre with her tied to it. They'd lost their quarry once, they wouldn't take the chance she'd get away again.

She also couldn't be seen entering Heloise's house. Her friend hadn't gotten away scot-free. Because she'd been such close friends with Isabeau, she'd been locked in her room since Isabeau disappeared. She'd only managed to sneak out that very night.

The idiot girl had run straight to Rudolph's house, hoping to reconcile with her betrothed. He hadn't so much as tried to see her since the whole incident. Heloise had been hurt and shocked, but assumed she'd be able to convince him of her innocence.

Instead, she'd found him beating up the town whore. Isabeau winced for poor Clarabelle. Her fall from grace had more to do with the death of her husband than a promiscuous nature. She'd been left alone and penniless. Having narrowly avoided a similar fate, Isabeau could definitely sympathize.

But she couldn't be sorry Heloise had been witness to that particular horror. She'd finally realized her fiancé wasn't the perfect man she'd always thought. And his downfall was Isabeau's gain. Heloise might not have forgiven Isabeau so readily if she hadn't had such recent proof of her fiancé's perverse personality.

A flicker of light appeared across the street. That was the signal she'd been waiting for. Everyone in the house but Heloise was sound asleep.

Unease made Isabeau hesitate. What if it were a trap? What if Heloise's parents had caught her sneaking home and forced her to tell them what she'd been doing? Or worse, what if Heloise had only pretended to believe Isabeau? She'd betrayed her once before, would she do it again?

Zut alors!

If only they could do this somewhere else. But no, Heloise insisted the spell must be cast near the area where Isabeau had disappeared if she wanted to return to the same time. Isabeau knew she was right, she just didn't like it.

The light still shone from across the street. She pushed away from the wall. Better to run or walk? Running would draw more attention, but walking would keep her out in the open that much longer.

She'd run. Better chance of getting across the street before throwing up. She scanned the street once more. Nothing. No movement, no sound.

One deep breath. Another. One more. She screwed up her courage. On three. One. Two. Three.

****

The candles cast an eerie glow over the hospital room. Sherri looked even more haggard. Her head tilted forward, but she managed to stay upright in the visitor's chair he'd moved to the center of the room. Guilt continued to gnaw at Gray's stomach. Then he thought of Isabeau. Alone. Stranded at who knew what point in time.

"We need to start now."

He jerked in surprise. He'd thought she'd fallen asleep again, but she sat straight, a concerned frown on her face. He didn't like the urgency of her tone. "Why? What's wrong? Are you okay? Should I call in the nurse?" He half stood, ready to sprint for the door if she needed help.

"No. It's not that." She shook her head, her eyes squinted half shut. "I'm just suddenly feeling like we have to do this now. I don't know why."

Could she have more witch in her than he'd thought? Maybe her blood was showing through years of suppression. If so, what did this mean for Isabeau? "Has something happened? Is she in trouble?"

"I don't think so. I just feel a sense of urgency. It's strange."

"Let's get started then." He handed her Uncle Stan's book, open to the page with the spell. "Let me cast the protective circle. As soon as it's complete, read that page."

He peered over her shoulder to read how to cast the magick circle. "Walk deosil… What's that?"

"Clockwise." Sherri appeared as surprised at her answer as he felt. "How did I know that? I can't remember ever hearing that word before."

It must be a sign, right? "Magick is in your blood.

Maybe that's proof." He straightened, lit the herbs he'd collected before coming and made a clockwise circle around Sherri.

They both gasped when a circle of silver sparkles lit up the room before quickly fading away.

"Holy shit." Excitement made his pulse skyrocket. This could work.

It had to.

****

Isabeau dashed across the road, her breathing overloud in her ears. Her hands shook so much she knew she'd never get the door open.

Thankfully, she didn't have to. Heloise slipped out with a finger to her lips for silence. She jerked her chin toward the steps that led to her cellar.

How were they going to lift the heavy wooden door without making a racket?

Heloise handed the candle—in a beautiful silver holder Isabeau had once tried using to fend off Rudolph all those years ago—to Isabeau. The cloth sack she had over her shoulder slipped to the ground by the basement entrance. She flicked the latch on the cellar door and swung it open with an ear-piercing shriek.

She and Heloise stood stock still, listening for any answering noise or signs of alarm. Several agonizing seconds later, Heloise grabbed her bag and they proceeded to the cellar.

The bag contained a dozen beeswax candles. Expensive stuff. Even Heloise's family used tallow most of the time. Heloise risked her father's wrath if he found out. Luckily, her mother was a pushover and would never begrudge her daughter a little extra light. Of course, not if the light were being used to cast a spell. Not even Heloise's mother could overlook the devil's work. She would have had a fit if she'd realized it was her own mother who taught Heloise and Isabeau the craft.

Placing and lighting the candles took only a few minutes. Isabeau wrinkled her nose at the damp, musty scent of the cellar. Mixed with the wax's pleasant odor, she didn't know whether to breathe deep or sneeze.

At long last, they were ready. Isabeau chose to create her own protective circle. Yes, she'd decided she could trust Heloise to help her, but she wasn't taking any unnecessary chances. Not this time.

Heloise sat on a barrel against the far wall, while Isabeau made her clockwise turn around the circle of candles. A satisfying glimmer of silver sparkles let her know when her ring of safety was complete. Isabeau sat on the barrel they'd placed in the center of the circle.

"Now what do we do?" she asked Heloise.

"Focus on your desire to return to your man. Then cast your spell. If he, in turn, searches for you, the spell will push you toward him."

"And if he's not looking for me?"

Heloise frowned. "I don't know."

"You don't know?" Isabeau shuddered. All the possibilities swirled through her mind. Most of them weren't good.

****

Gray nodded to Sherri to recite the spell. It sounded like poetic nonsense to him, but he had faith in his uncle and aunt's research. Uncle Stan wouldn't have left the information for Isabeau if he wasn't damn sure it would work. He would never do anything to harm someone he cared about.

Please. Please let this work.

The sage burned in its little silver dish, a plume of smoke rising toward the ceiling. Right toward the fire alarm. Shit. He grabbed the dish and moved it to the floor near Sherri's feet. Then he grabbed some of his uncle's papers and used them as a fan to waft the smoke away from the smoke detector. Setting off the alarm was not in his plans.

Sherri's voice wavered as she recited the spell for a second time.

"Hear these words, hear our cry,
spirits from the other side.
We seek your help for one we've lost,
for her safe return, we'll bear the cost.
Return her to us from days gone by,
to the home she loves where safety lie.
We've had our say, you've heard our plea,
if it please, so mote it be."

He whispered the words along with her, while continuously scanning the room. Searching for any sign that what they were doing was having an effect. Surely something should have happened by now? His uncle's notes didn't say anything about having to repeat the spell over and over.

Sherri's voice faltered, but she continued her refrain.

"Sherri. Stop." He couldn't let her go on. She had a newborn to take care of. She'd already been through enough today and he'd piled onto her stress.

Her voice dropped off, the last line a mere whisper, "…so mote it be."

He tapped the sage against its plate until the fire went out, sending little puffs of smoke throughout the room. Then he blew out all the candles. He spent a minute fanning the air to clear the room of smoke. Sherri barely moved. He'd have to help her so she could get some proper sleep.

"Come on. Let's get you back into bed."

Once he had her settled in, he gathered up all his supplies in a plastic bag and turned to leave.

"I'm sorry," Sherri said seconds before her head fell to the side and her breathing evened out into the soft snoring of a deep sleep.

"I'm sorry, too," he whispered as he let himself out of her room. Tears burned his eyes. He could barely make out the nurses' shocked faces as he passed. They must not have realized he was there. One woman rushed into Sherri's room.

Good. He wanted someone to check on her. He'd never forgive himself if something happened to her. And for what?

Nothing.

He'd failed.

Isabeau was lost to him forever.

Chapter Twelve

Isabeau blinked at the fluorescent hospital lights' glare. Her heart skipped a beat. Yes. Electricity. She'd moved forward in time again.

But how far? Had she truly returned to Gray? Or would she find him only to discover he was only three years old? Or sixteen? Or seventy?

She stared around the deserted hospital corridor. Everything appeared the same as she'd seen it last, though she could see it was nighttime through the glass doors at the end.

She had to find Gray. That was the only way she'd know for sure. Surely the spell wouldn't have worked if he weren't searching for her.

If he didn't want her.

Her stomach griped at her, queasiness made her dizzy. She hadn't eaten all day. She wouldn't be able to stomach anything at the moment, but having an empty stomach didn't help her feel any better.

Maybe she should test her boundaries first? She turned away from the doors and scrutinized the spot where she'd traveled earlier that day. Only a dozen feet and she'd know whether she was here to stay.

They were the most difficult steps she'd ever taken. Hesitant at first, she put on a burst of speed for the last few to make sure she didn't lose her nerve.

And sailed right past. She spun in a circle, a quick

laugh escaping her before she could squelch it. No more fear of falling upon a new cursed spot and having to start over again and again. She could travel, she could go anywhere she wished.

But she didn't want to do any of those things without Gray. He'd become her reason for staying in one time. Her anchor. She had to find him.

Home first. That seemed the most logical. She thought through all the places they'd been, planning her search order as she left the hospital.

"Woof."

Havoc barreled into her, nearly knocking her to the ground with his enthusiastic greeting. He leaned his weight against her, his tail wagging a mile a minute. He shoved his muzzle into her hand. His cold, wet nose brought her back to her senses. She'd gone on instinct and braced herself to stay upright. Now she bent over and wrapped her arms around the dog. "Havoc. It's so good to see you, boy. What are you doing here?"

"He's with me."

Her heart leaped into her throat. Gray's voice washed over her. She closed her eyes. Tears threatened.

She straightened and slowly turned to face him. He took her breath away. Rumpled and tired, but oh so sexy. His clothes were wrinkled and his short hair stuck out all over the place like he'd been running his hands through it. His glasses lay crooked on the bridge of his nose.

He looked like he'd missed her.

She stood there like a dolt. She wanted to fling herself into his arms, but nerves held her back. What if his feelings weren't the same as hers? The spell had worked, so he must have searched for her. But why?

Because he loved her? Or because he felt too guilty not to? He was a decent person. No matter how he felt about her, he wouldn't let her disappear without at least trying to get her back.

"Damn, Isabeau. Say something. Please. I was an asshole. I'm sorry. Tell me you forgive me. Or tell me I'm an asshole, but that I at least have a chance at making it up to you. Tell me you return even half the feelings I have for you. I can work with that. I never would have been able to forgive myself if you'd disappeared forever. I love you."

Her mouth dropped open. Her heartbeat soared. "I-I love you, too."

They came together instantly. His hands tangled in her hair, his mouth caressed hers. She sighed in bliss. She couldn't get enough. She wrapped her arms around him, her heart resting against his chest. The heat of his body burned away the chill that had encompassed her for most of the day.

Havoc bumped against the backs of her knees, almost bringing both of them to the ground.

Gray laughed. "I believe Havoc approves."

Isabeau stared at the dog for a second, getting a sense of what her familiar wanted. She nodded. "He does. But he also thinks we should take this somewhere a little more private."

The sweetness of Gray's kiss made her melt against him. She was lucky he kept a steadying hand on her waist when he pulled away or she might have fallen over. Her legs had turned to mush.

"I agree," he said. "Let's go home."

Home. She liked the sound of that.

A word about the author...

Emma Kaye is married to her high school sweetheart and has two beautiful kids that she spends an insane amount of time driving around central New Jersey.

Before ballet classes and tennis entered her life, she decided to write one of those romances she loved to read and discovered a new passion. She has been writing ever since.

Add in a hyper dog and an extremely patient cat and she's living her own happily ever after while making her characters work hard to reach theirs. Emma's time-travel romance, *Time for Love*, is also available at The Wild Rose Press.

http://emma-kaye.com